Home Fires

HOME FIRES

Jean Rysstad

HARBOUR PUBLISHING

Harbour Publishing
P.O. Box 219, Madeira Park, BC Canada V0N 2H0

Published with the assistance of the Canada Council and the
Government of British Columbia, Cultural Services Branch.

Cover painting by Gaye Hammond
Cover design by Roger Handling, Terra Firma Design
Author photo by Nancy Robertson
Printed and bound in Canada

Canadian Cataloguing in Publication Data

Rysstad, Jean, 1949–
        Home fires

        ISBN 1-55017-159-3

        I. Title.
PS8585.Y88H6 1997   C813'54   C97-910123-9
PR9199.3.R97H6 1997

To the family, east and west

Contents

Houselife

It is Hallowe'en night. Joe is downtown at the Sea-View Hotel playing to what is probably a full house. Both the hour and the night are right for a full house. He does a single, plays guitar, sits on a green leather-topped stool we brought from the old house in Saskatchewan.

I have the radio tuned, at low volume, to CBC as I begin to mark twenty college student papers. The assignment: Write about a house.

Arthur Black broadcasts live from a small Nova Scotian town that wishes to remain anonymous, as do the people living in a huge old house there. In the wee hours, Black explains, a medium will arrive to exorcise ghosts from this house.

The woman who lives there describes sitting in the tub one day, the water at half-full mark. Her left arm rested on the edge of the tub. Five drops of water appeared on her dry arm. The ceiling did not leak and besides, it hadn't rained for days. She brushed the water off her arm and felt her hair being yanked. Another day, while she was bathing, drops fell on her left knee. She felt a finger touch her leg and then her back, three times. Now she's talking about noises behind the mirror, and I reach behind me and shut the radio off.

The house in this student's paper is huge. It's got high ceilings and a banister of "light coloured wood." ("I don't know the name of this wood," the student writes in brackets. I write "oak?" in red pen.) There's a beautiful view and a brass knocker and a fireplace, which makes the living room cozy. There is love all over the house, she writes. It's evident in the polished furniture, which is carved, handmade. Another student's house is also huge and old, but the paint is chipped and it's cold and the furniture is shabby. "Looks like it came from or should go to the dump. It's gross." The wind blows right through the cracks in the walls where dead spiders hang in stringy webs. Only two of the twenty students admire glass and plush white carpets.

I make a cup of tea and decide against having even half of one of the chocolate big-foot donuts in the paper bag on the drainboard in the kitchen. This is an old house with high ceilings. We rent. The sink is too low for me, and I am the Canadian average height, 5'4". Our landlady, who had the house built for her, is short. The house I grew up in, in Ontario, had the same white porcelain low sink but we had a pump too. It was painted hooker's green. In dry weather it had to be primed. It wheezed. The pump water came from a concrete cistern, a vat of dark rain water in the basement. We all used this "soft" water with spiders' legs spinning in it for hair washing. We had tap water too, and when I filled the tub, running hot and cold together, I used to hear voices babbling.

My parents did not argue often and never loudly, but

when there was tension in the house, I couldn't sleep. I would sit in the stairwell waiting for the air to change: just a hint of a laugh from my mother would be enough. Often but not always in that house, I would feel as though I were looking down on myself, over my own shoulder. The last time it happened was when I was home from university for a weekend. I felt a layer of me lift and rush up from my toes—I would have gone travelling, but the rest of me, especially my head, put the brakes on—and that sensation of leaving myself has never come back to me. I would not want it to.

When I first came west I lived alone in a third-storey apartment on Main Street. It was an old building with high ceilings, the walls white plaster, the floors wooden. Porcelain sinks and tub. Once, when I was in the tub, shaving my legs, I looked up and saw a shabbily dressed stranger looking down at me. He had silently opened my door, and must have heard water and turned toward the sound. In a voice I didn't recognize as my own, I told him to leave. Get out. He said he was sorry. He stood stammering, babbling apologies. "Get out," I said again, "or I'll call the police." He vanished. The door shut and I heard him outside saying again, "I'm sorry." Wrapped in a towel, I threw the deadbolt and in my own voice repeated, "Go away or I'll call the police."

Joe and I left Prince Rupert with everything we owned in a 1957 yellow school bus. The seats had been removed and a dry sink set in a little wooden cupboard. There were green terrycloth curtains, faded and water-stained, over the windows. Joe drove and I sat beside him in a captain's chair. We had a mattress on top of the furniture, books, clothes, amplifiers and speaker columns. When we lay down on the mattress, we could not stretch up our arms. If we bent our knees they would bump the inside of the curving roof. We both wore olive green gas attendant suits with red plaid flannel lining. The bus had no heat. It was November 2nd. We left early evening and drove ninety miles inland, to Terrace. We had money because the fishing season had been good for Joe and the waitress season goes accordingly. We got a motel and went to a schnitzel house on the Terrace highway. Joe had a mooseburger and I had Vienna schnitzel. We drank a bottle of wine and lingered over coffee, then moved to the lounge for last call. It was a hunter's lounge with stuffed animals and birds perched on the slab cedar coffee tables. Deer and moose and fox eyes stared dreamily from all the panelled walls.

The next day, as we travelled east to southern Saskatchewan, I read to Joe from Norman Mailer's *The Executioner's Song*. Sandi, the bartender at the Surf Club, had lent it to me when she finally finished it, after reading it for weeks during slack early evening hours. I read at night, holding a flashlight in one hand as we rolled along and upward. I could not put down the story of those two people, Gary Gilmore and Nicole. He gets out of prison, still a young man, but a man who's been in trouble for most of his life. And although his mother's Mormon family offer him a job and sympathy, a second chance, and although you hope for him, and you know Nicole loves him deeply, you know she's deeply screwed up too. Gary will murder. He knows. Nicole knows and we knew. Each page brought us closer to knowing why. It was just a matter of when and how; the end of the story was our destination.

We bought a bottle of rum when we hit Medicine Hat. Filled up our two thermoses with coffee at

Somebody's Pancake House, baskets of twigs hanging in the McDonald's-like arches. Joe wanted to drive straight through to Kincaid, the little village we were moving to. He talked about the place, told me how he loved the old house we were to live in. It cost $10,000 in that small town and would have been ten times as much in Prince Rupert. He wondered about transporting part of the house back to Rupert on a trailer, tearing down the rest for materials, then rebuilding. Could it be done? Some part of him wanted to bring that house home, rather than call the house home where it was.

I could write about that house. Front door and back door stories. I could write something about each of the floors (four), and each of the rooms. I brought our first baby home to that house from the Moose Jaw hospital. The day Julie first smiled, I ran with her in my arms down to the basement, where my mother was painting a little iron stool she'd found behind the furnace.

A month later, on a spring day when I had all the doors wide open for the sweet air to blow through, an old woman appeared in the kitchen while I was bathing the baby in a basin on the table. She must have knocked or called out at the front door, and maybe again as she came through the sun porch and the dining room, but I didn't hear her.

She was tall. She was dressed for visiting in a flowery spring dress, a black pocketbook in the crook of one arm. She held a bouquet of white lilacs. "I'm Mrs. Swanson," she said, "and I'm ninety-two and don't put the kettle on. I don't drink tea. I just talk." She touched the baby's cheek. "Oh, dear new wee life," she said, and sat down.

She talked and talked and talked. She knew this house so well and loved it well. It was time someone made it a home again. Would I lead a group of young girls, take on Canadian Girls In Training? Explorers? Sunday School? What would or could I do to make the village home?

I don't know how long we'll be staying, I kept saying, at first gently and then insistent until she heard me. She became distant then, cool, when she'd been so warm and welcoming. She said the doctor gave her pills to slow down her mind but she didn't and wouldn't take them. There wasn't time.

It began to blow like the prairie storms I'd read about but never seen, and all the doors slammed shut. Outside was a blur of sand and dust. "I must go home," Mrs. Swanson said.

I knew I would never see her again but that she and her invitation would always haunt me: a tall old woman struggling against time, so little left and so much to be done before the earth blew away. I watched her go head first into the brown wind, her skirt blown hard against her stockinged legs.

The house is a state of mind, and it sighs. Content or restless. Last year, Joe was still fishing on Hallowe'en night, and I was almost religiously content. The phone rang at eleven and it was Joe's mom calling about pajamas she was making from this wonderful warm flannelette, striped and thick. She couldn't sleep and she was sewing in her upstairs alcove. Could I find a tape measure and imagine my son, stand him there in front of me, and measure him? I balanced the receiver on my ear while reaching for the sewing tin, stuffed full of thread and needles. I'd been there for supper, to Joe's folks' huge old house, gone down the cedared path in the rainy darkness, a kid in each hand. Tidy golden dollars, pancakes, and duva—

deer meat and drippings—fried in the iron pan, butter and garlic salt, the loin, sliced thin with the sharp fillet knife. Sat hungry-irritable on the kitchen bench seat, leafing through *Westcoast Fisherman* magazines stacked in the corner. Finally we jabbed forks into the fry pan set out as a common dish.

Jokes about fork-wounds flew over the kids, who were smug in the knowledge of their value. We left warm and full but I was glad to be going home. Was glad for the connection with Joe's mother at eleven o'clock and with Joe, an hour later, when he called from the boat.

Write about a house, I told my students. Anything about a house that you feel or sense, dream, remember. With grade six students I once used shoes: some from our shelf, some from the Salvation Army. I told them to put themselves into a shoe. One boy wrote about an unemployed slipper. The red plaid size 12 shuffled about as it fried an egg halfway through the morning. The man in the slipper pushed his plate away without eating and stood at the window for a long time staring at the trees.

We trick-or-treated earlier tonight. Julie was a butterfly and Jeremy was Superman. I try to keep their houselife free from horrors, monsters, ban G.I. Joe and Masters of the Universe. Just when I thought they were both asleep, I heard footsteps and knew it would be Julie. "There's ghosts in my room," she said. I took her back upstairs, tucked her in. Told her: think good things. Don't bug me any more. You had a good night. Don't push it.

But for a year she had dreams I could not dismiss. The dreams made me think of *The Shining*, the hotel in the movie version which looks like the Banff Springs Hotel, the word REDRUM written in blood, the child who rode the halls on his tricycle. Every time Julie cried out from her upstairs bedroom, the sound more a grunt than a cry, I would go to the stairs and see her cringing at the top. I would say to her and to myself as I went up slowly, say over and over, "It's okay."

She could not see or recognize me, though her eyes were open and she called for me. It seemed each way she turned there was a hand reaching for her, a hand that offered only horror. I would find a voice somewhere that was calm, not fearful, sit on the step just below the landing and ask her to come, take her wrists firmly, take her on my knee as she fought me, then carry her downstairs to the couch, sit with her, rock the struggling little person I didn't know, who didn't know me, until she fell asleep.

It is two o'clock now. I can easily imagine that I just felt one small tug at the back of my sweater. Joe may walk in the door at any moment. He may be wearing the Ronald Reagan mask his brother lent him just in case he felt like performing in costume.

Julie's dreams didn't happen often, but I mentioned the first one to the family doctor. He said all children have nightmares. The books and articles I read distinguished between nightmares and night terrors. "It may be that there is tension in the home or that the child is over-stimulated," *Children's Magazine* offered. A child psychiatrist said: "A child's life *should* be slightly boring. If a child is having sleep problems, the parents should ask themselves what they can do to reduce stress and make life calmer."

After one of Julie's dreams, when she was coming out of the state, she said: "I hate... I hate..." I ventured: "Is it me you hate?" She shuddered. "No," she said. "No."

I felt I was on the track of something that, thank God, was not ghosts but only houselife. The next time I went to see the doctor it was for Julie's earache, but I decided to ask again. Probe again. I told him it was the same dream, a recurring dream, and that it was something to do with me. He said mothers always assume guilt. He asked if we had a violent houselife. If Joe had ever hit me. "Never," I said. "but we're vocal when we fight. It clears the air." The doctor said I had to be open, had to open my mind to possibilities, that another reason for recurring dreams is that the child has been molested. He said I would find a clue.

I told Joe what the doctor said.

That very night, she had a dream. I was amazed, now that I knew a little about "terrors," how much like the book descriptions they were, right down to the time they occur—in the first hours of sleep. I went to Julie and carried her down to the couch in the living room. We snuggled under a crocheted blanket, and after the "fit" was over, I told her: "I can't help you if you won't tell me. Is someone hurting you? Is a man hurting you?" She nodded. "Will you tell me who?"

"No," she said. "I can't."

I started naming babysitters, neighbours, boys I'd seen in the alley. Each name brought a no from Julie. And so I had to go in close and it felt so bad I had to whisper. Uncle? Grandpa? No, No. "It's Daddy," she said. My throat went dry.

"Daddy's hurting *you*," she said.

I felt faint with relief, dizzy and swirling, and then a kind of grounding, an acceptance, a pride in our house, our lives, how intimately and inescapably connected we are.

"He climbs on you and beats you up. I'm afraid he'll kill you," she said.

"Dad and Mom—it's something like wrestling or

playing, what we do at night. And even when you hear us fighting, it's part of love. Even not-loving is part of loving."

"Daddy's stronger," Julie said, a bit doubtful, but her voice was happier.

"In some ways," I said. "But don't worry. You don't need to worry. I'm strong too."

She fell asleep, her head in my lap.

Joe winced in pain when I told him about the dream and the conversation, the uncovering. I felt joyous, really felt like dancing a jig.

November 1st: a trail of peanut shells and two Chiclet boxes from the front door to the back. Houselife.

Plus Minus Interesting

The kids left on Sunday for a three-week holiday with their grandmother and today, Tuesday, I now have a sense of what life will be like without them.

Can I have two dollars for gum. Two dollars? Since when does gum cost two dollars? Oh. Special sports gum that releases energy into the body. Go. Take the money. Whose turn is it to feed the dog? To do dishes? No one speaks. I will take this damn dog back to the SPCA and she will find a home with kids who love her. Who's going to hold the bag and who's going to shovel the poop on the lawn into it? I did it last time. Yes, it stinks. You guys work it out. I don't care. Just do it. A test tomorrow? Why do you wait till 10:30 to tell me you don't understand your algebra? Where's my mascara? At school. Please don't take my things.

I miss them.

This morning while I was making the bed, I heard the most desolate wailing. I pulled back the curtain and stared across the street at a little boy, four or five years old, a red helmet on his head. He was sprawled on the curb, crying, his bike with a pink flag on top of him. His dad, a young man who looked like he'd just started shaving in the last year or two, crossed over to our side of the street when the boy began to cry. He kept on walking. "You little suck," the father said, "get up on your feet. Get up." And the boy screamed, "I hate you, I hate you," as the dad ignored him, walked on.

I wanted to take that boy in my arms and wipe his tears, walk on his side of the street, follow behind him calling, "Wow! You're doing good, you little hot shot!"

I don't remember many words of wisdom from the Bible but this proverb for parents has arrived: Do not provoke your children.

I resolve: I will not provoke my children even when they are provoking me. I will bite my tongue until it bleeds. I will not laugh even to ease the pain when I am stabbed with a truth or near-truth. I will take the dog for a walk. We both need the exercise. I will listen to the lyrics of *Nirvana Unplugged*; I will listen to Hole and Green Day and the Cranberries and remember my mother sitting on the edge of my bed in my basement room, circa 1965, listening to me sing "Sometimes I Feel Like a Motherless Child" all those years ago. She didn't laugh. Maybe the song hurt her. She didn't flinch.

Lately I've been wishing I could have one more child. It would be interesting to see how this child would turn out, surrounded by two teens and a mom and dad who know the ropes. What is the ideal product? A faith in the family, a shot or two of wariness, and the resilience to recover when hurt and to resist or flee when necessary?

Yesterday at Green Apple Fish & Chips I saw a newborn swaddled in an expensive buggy. This kid had a head full of black hair and a whole whack of it stuck straight up like it had been jelled that way. Each time the door opened his black down swayed. His starry black eyes turned to the wind of this world with wonder, without fear. I wished he were mine.

One night a few weeks ago when Jeremy was out playing street hockey, Julie, Joe and I sat down to supper. Joe and Julie each reviewed their day and what was ahead for the evening and the next morning. Then I told them about my day. I'd gone to the grocery store and had encountered a mother and daughter in the bakery section. The girl was about six, and she sat in the buggy seat. She was too big for the buggy, was old enough to walk on her own two feet and behave, but instead, she grasped and grabbed at things on the shelves. When the mother tried to put an item back, the girl hung on tight, yelling, "I want it, I want it!" The mother was flushed but she struggled to stay calm, and she gave in several times.

It bothered me, so I steered my cart away from them. The next time I saw mom and little girl, they were in checkout #2. I chose #3 even though it was a longer line-up. Here was another mother, with three young children: a baby asleep in its car seat which was set down in the buggy, a toddler set up on the cheque-writing ledge, and an older boy of four or so waiting patiently by his mom's side even though he did not have a very good view of things from down there.

The toddler on the ledge was the I-missed-my-nap kind of tired and cranky, whimpering, jerking this way and that while his mother tried to write the cheque. She pressed him against her body with her one free hand, but he broke free and flailed at her face. She caught him tight again and finished writing. The cashier dipped into her bucket of balloons and offered one to the boy but he whipped his head away from her and struck his face on his mother's cheekbone. He began to scream. I thought it must have hurt the mom too but she was stoic.

The cashier and I gave the mother sympathetic grimaces, and we watched as the four of them wheeled out the door. Then we turned our attention to the action in the next checkout. The big little girl in the buggy had a treat in each hand but she was tortured by the huge display of chocolate bars and gum. "I want... I want..."

"I don't know why today's so bad," the cashier said as she scanned my groceries. "Every kid that's been in has been miserable. Usually you can cheer them up. Not today."

"So," I said to Julie, "watching those two mothers today brought back the days when you and Jeremy were little. That mom with the three kids, next time she might want to wait an hour before she goes shopping, let her babes have their naps. And the other one, she should have taken that six-year-old home the minute she started acting like a spoiled brat. I remember once when you and I and Jeremy were in the drug store and you were about four, Julie—"

"Drug store," Julie said. "I remember that time. I loved that drug store. There were three aisles of toys. My Little Ponies and dolls that talked and all the Fisher-Price stuff."

"Yeah," I said, "and one day you wanted a pony or something and I put it back on the shelf and you laid down on the floor and started screaming. I just left my cart in the aisle and took you to the car, and you screamed all the way home but you didn't do that again."

"No..." Julie said, tentative at first. Then: "No! You pulled my pants down and spanked me in the store. And—"

"I did *not!*" I said.

Joe, who'd been tapping the end of the ketchup bottle with his knife, gave it a final thunk. He looked from Julie to me and back to Julie to see if either of us might lighten up at the sight of the big glop of red on his plate, but it was too late.

"I have never, never pulled your pants down in public and I don't think I ever even spanked you in public." I said this fiercely and finally because there was no doubt. Julie was wrong. Screwed up memories. Jeez. "Jeez," I said. "Julie!"

She has huge eyes, and her tears when they gather and sit on the eyeballs seem about a quarter of an inch thick. They splash when they fall. "Yes," she said. "Yes..." slowly but much more sure. "Well, maybe not that time but when we lived in that brick house you spanked me and Jeremy all the time. You spanked us really hard with our pants down."

"You kids hardly ever got spanked. Hardly ever," Joe said calmly between bites.

"I wish Jer was home," Julie said. "He knows. We talk about it sometimes. Just ask him."

"I've heard you guys laughing about how Dad spanked. How he would use this big bad roar and you'd be so scared and then he'd give you a gentle tap. How you guys had to hide your faces to keep from laughing. I've heard you say I was the one you were afraid of."

"Because you *hurt* us," Julie said.

"Once or twice," I said. "Once or twice when you kids were acting like such brats I couldn't stand it any more. But c'mon. It's not like you had this monster for a mother. Get real."

By then, both Joe and I were inspecting Julie like she was insane, maybe. A stranger to us, certainly.

"Quit!" she yelled. "Don't look at me. I hate it when you do that," and she pushed herself back from the table and ran upstairs.

After a moment I went to the stairs, called Julie to come back to us. She took her time and held her head high as she entered the kitchen.

"I'm sorry," I said. "I can't change what your memories are but I want you to know with my whole heart and memory that I never spanked you often and never in public."

"Stop talking about it," Julie said as she cut pieces of cake for all of us.

I could not leave it alone. "I started to tell you guys about what happened at the grocery store but that was just part one of what I was going to say before we got side-tracked."

I teach a class of adult students how to write compositions, and I use current events as journal topic start-ups, so every night I go through the newspapers looking for subjects. Then, to get them thinking about their topics, I use Edward de Bono's Plus Minus Interesting exercise. First you take a position such as "All cars should be painted yellow," and you force yourself to think of all the good reasons to support that position (+). Next you set those thoughts aside and come up with as many arguments as you can against the position (-). Finally you list everything about it that you find interesting. The students work in groups of five or six, and the whole process takes about ten minutes. In that short time you get a glimpse of your own prejudices, and your emotional resistance to the other side. Plus, you get an insight into how PMI affects others.

So, the day I was in the grocery store, I'd taken a clipping to class about an American couple and their children, aged three and five, on a driving holiday. The family had stopped in at a McDonald's for lunch. It was hot. The kids were getting antsy in the back seat and the dad warned the older child to stop bugging the younger. When the child got out of the car, she deliberately, according to the father, slammed the door on her brother's fingers. The father lost it. He grabbed the little girl, laid her over the hood of the car, pulled down her pants and gave her approximately five good whacks. A woman who had seen the incident called the police and the man was charged with abuse or cruelty or something like that. The girl's buttocks were examined and no physical scars were found. The man was tried and acquitted. He admitted that he'd lost his temper, and said he would do the same thing again but not in public.

My students and I read the article together and decided the PMI position would be: Spanking should be illegal. Some of these adult students have had hard lives, have survived abuse, violence or neglect. Others claim their leaving school or breaking the law or screwing up is entirely their own fault. But every one of them thought the judge's verdict had been right, the father should have been acquitted. Parents have the right and responsibility to discipline their children when words haven't worked. Spanking is not abuse. Obviously.

"Acquitted?" Julie said.

"We looked it up," I said. "It means not guilty even though it sounds like a guilty word. Quit. Stop it.

Anyway," I said, "we ran out of time, but I was still thinking about it when I got to the store, and I guess that's why I was watching those mothers and their kids so closely."

By this time, Joe had left us and hit the couch. Julie said she might be wrong about being spanked bare bottom in the store or on the street. She said she might have some things mixed up with Oprah and also with the McDonald's incident, which her class had talked about that day too, in Humanities.

"But you *were* mean sometimes," she said. "I'm not going to spank my kids," she said as she scraped the icing off the cake knife with her thumb. "There's lots of ways around it. I know from babysitting. You can mostly distract kids, show them something else to do."

I gave her thumb a little snick as she licked the icing. She ignored me. "It's hard," she said. "It's so complicated because *I* lose it all the time. I get so mad at everyone at home. But never when I'm babysitting."

We had a long hug.

After dinner, Julie went biking for a while with a friend and I did the dishes. When she came in, she said she couldn't stop thinking about the topic, that it led into False Memory Syndrome and True Memories. "Even if your memories aren't true, if you *feel* them, they must be *sort* of true," she said. "It would be awful to have nobody believe you. It would be the worst. But it would be awful to be found guilty if it weren't true and have nobody believe you."

Silence.

"I think I'd like to be a judge," Julie said. "I think I'd make an excellent judge."

Jeremy came home, went straight for the fridge and then to the TV. Beavis and Butt-head. Julie and I moved in on him. I turned the volume down on the "huh-huh huh huh" guys. "What do you like about that show?" I asked him.

"The music," he said.

"The music and...?"

"They're so stupid they're funny," he said. "You should watch it sometime."

"Jer," I said, "did you get spanked a lot when you were younger?"

He studied my face as I had known he would, but I didn't give him anything to go on. He looked at Julie. No clues from her either. He was out on a limb and he jumped off.

"Well, yeah," he said. "You spanked hard. I was scared of you when you got mad."

"Did I ever spank you on the street, pull your pants down on the street?"

"I remember once you stopped the car and pulled our pants down and spanked us both. It really hurt. We cried for a long time. 'Member, Julie? It was when we lived in that crooked house where the marbles ran down to the walls. We had races with them to see whose would get to the door first."

Julie frowned, thinking, trying to remember it.

"Jeez," I said, trying to be funny. "I hope you guys aren't gonna carry this thing around with you your whole lives. It's not like I used a wooden spoon or a belt or—"

"Oh yeah," said Julie, quick, coming at me with a big grin. "What about that dungeon you used to lock us up in? And the chains?"

"Whips," Jer said.

"And that time you fed us bread and water for a week."

"Shaved our heads," said Jer.

We were all laughing then and that was the end. It was a good ending, sort of. They were teasing me. We were playing. But it's eerie too. How quick they were with details.

And how just this morning, when I wanted to run out and hug that boy sprawled on the sidewalk, I suddenly remembered being stretched like a rubber band, alone with the kids on maybe the sixth week of herring season, Joe gone, nonstop rain and wind, dead battery in the car, no money in the bank, no fish in the net. I remembered this little boy, my own four-year-old, coming down from his bedroom for the tenth time in his flannel pj's imprinted with trucks or cars, to whine about something. Maybe he was hot. Maybe he was cold. I remembered the rage that rose in me as I chased him, grabbed his little arms as he scrambled up the stairs to get away from me. I remembered how he dropped, collapsed into a somnolence, a trancelike state, right there on the third step, and how the charge of anger that had built up in me over the weeks flashed and emptied the second I saw this—my own little pale boy sinking as far back as he could into himself and safety.

Sometime I'll ask him about it. I'll tell him my version: I *did* take him in my arms, kiss him, tuck him back into bed, but he played dead, and I love his little large soul for that. I mean, I respect his instinct and his pride.

So: There's one more thing for the PMI. It's interesting how "private" vs. "public" becomes the defence. As if "losing it" at home is a hundred percent better than "losing it" in public. Why?

Romeos

Susan has holes in her heart and thinks maybe in her head too but she's as happy today as she's been for years. It's Easter Monday and she's heard Curly's in town, has bought a boat, is licensed for the herring. The northern fishery is a bit late this year and the fleet is just hanging around waiting for the word: Opening.

Toby, Susan's six-year-old, is sitting beside her in the yellow Datsun, seatbelt buckled. He's wearing the plastic cowboy hat he got for ten cents at his school's garage sale, the size 6x jeans with the patch on the knee, twenty-five cents, and a tan-coloured sweater with real tanned leather insets that he spotted himself on a hanger in the gym that day—also twenty-five cents.

Susan likes worn things, she likes recycling, reviving, but sometimes she forks out a lot of money for Oshkosh B'Gosh. Then she kicks herself and wants to rip off the designer label with the cute words that cost so much.

Susan and Toby live alone. Toby's dad, Susan's ex, has been living with another woman for about a year now, and they have a new baby. The woman—get this—was six months pregnant when Susan's ex took off. So yeah, there's holes in her head and in her heart. A few.

Oh well. She's haywired herself together, she's had to for Toby's sake. First she'd been so incensed—that's the word—steaming—that she'd gotten a lot accomplished. Gone back to school, gotten her upgrading and completed a six-credit course in "Addictions Counselling." She learned a lot, yeah. A lot about dependency, co-dependency, as they called it. And maybe she was *from* a dysfunctional family but damned if she was going to be in another one. And that term "Passive Aggression," was that ever a nail on the head. She's not quite so stunned now. She at least knows how to put names to some of the shit she's gone through.

But here she is in the Datsun in a tailwind or is it a tailspin, rushing down Cow Bay Road. Gliding, coasting. Her foot isn't even on the gas pedal. Curly's in town.

Susan heard from Marie that he was in Popeye's last night. Feeling no pain, Marie had said. Marie said he asked about her and what, she asked Marie, what exactly had he asked? He'd said: How's she doing, anyway? Susan couldn't get Marie to go any further. Marie's face had closed up and damned if Susan was going to beg for info or give any.

What is she doing gliding downhill toward him? She is not feather-brained any more. Curly is a bad actor. She just wants to have a laugh with him for old time's sake.

What matters now is that she keeps her head on straight for Toby, who's beside her singing "Crime of Passion"—only he thinks it's "Crime of Fashion" and she's never corrected him. The song's on a Ricky Van Shelton tape his dad left behind.

She turns up the volume and sings along with Ricky and Toby. How do you provide a little boy with a role model? She'd like to know the answer to that one. She'd seen Toby studying the picture of Ricky Van on the cassette jacket. He's slim and muscular, dressed in an undershirt and low-riding jeans, one leg slung over a straight-back chair. Of course he wears a white cowboy hat. Sometimes Susan feels like phoning her ex and yelling: For lack of a real man to imitate...

And Curly. His boat was called *Dancer*, he'd told Marie. The *Northern Dancer*. Good old Marie, she'd let that slip.

Susan expects the dock to be jammed with boats and aluminum punts but as they turn into the parking lot above the Cow Bay Fishing Company floats, she is surprised. There's no sea of masts and poles and wires, no ghetto blasters blasting. She lets the car roll to a stop, bump against the concrete abutment. She turns the key off and says, "Let's go, cowboy—I'll race you down the ramp."

There are only three gillnetters tied up and the *Northern Dancer*—a beamy old wooden boat—is one of them. She sees a padlock on the cabin door and her heart takes a little dip into disappointment. Oh well. So he isn't here. They'll wait. Half an hour maybe, no more.

Someone, not Curly, comes down the ramp. Susan and Toby follow his progress along the float, watch his wide-paced steps that are just right for the gaps where one float joins another. She and Toby had to take giant steps when they reached the gaps and her stomach spiralled, thinking what if Toby fell through?

"Excuse me," Susan says as the man walks by them. "Have you seen a guy—do you know the guy on the *Northern Dancer*? Have you seen him around?"

"He's around somewheres," the man says, eyeing her. "And he'll be taking off pretty quick when he gets here too," he adds suspiciously. As if she'll delay him. As if she's there to cause Curly pain. Susan reads these thoughts in the old fellow but then Toby, who's been hiding behind a big rusted oil drum heaped with net, appears beside her. The fellow warms.

"You the crew?" he asks Toby. "You going out fishing too?"

"*Can* I go fishing?" Toby asks after the man walks down the float to his own boat. "Who're we looking for, Mum?"

"An old friend," Susan says, poking a finger at Toby's tee-shirted torso. "Zip up your jacket. We're going to wait for him."

She lifts Toby from the float onto the deck of the *Dancer* and climbs over too. She tries the cabin door. Yeah, it's locked. She lifts the rain gear hanging on a hook by the door and finds two beer dangling from the six-pack plastic. Cold. She takes one and snaps the ring and pats the hold for Toby. "Come. Sit. Hop up," she says, offering her hand.

A breeze rustles in the alder trees and salal bushes above them in the parking lot and they both turn their faces to the wind. Susan takes a long cool drink of the beer and thinks herself down the road ahead. Some year, maybe next year, Curly, not the wind, will be ruffling Toby's hair... and...

Is she crazy? She must be just a little bit high from the beer. The top of her head feels like it's floating an inch or two above the rest of her. She should pull it down where it belongs, pull it on snug like a tuque. What is she doing here?

"How long are we waiting?" Toby asks.

A black and white cab noses into the parking lot and stops at the ramp. The passenger door falls open and because the car is on a downhill slope, the man falls with it.

It's Curly, Curly whose arm is stretched like an elastic when the heavy door falls away but Susan feels limp and tilted too.

Curly. Lax, relaxed, and... Susan stretches for words. Not *drunk*. She scrambles to find the handle for what he is and has always been. Lawless, a lawless body, lanky ragdoll man, a marionette. That line from Robert Frost: *Not like a man but a chandelier.*

Watching the whole picture of him is like watching clouds, the billowing kinds that change form and face and you find shapes turning to characters and dissolving into something else.

Two crew step out of the taxi and gather the gear, the duffel bags, the tie-down groceries from the trunk. They are straight-men, caretakers, wardens, burdens. What are they? They want something from Curly. They want to fish. They want to get going.

These thoughts thump in Susan as the three men come along the float in their romeos, their deck slippers, their pull-on leather boots. Thrrummp, thrrummp, thrrummp. They come like heartbeats, her thoughts. God, she wishes she could disappear or change shape now, change her face to save it. "Susan," she whispers to herself, "I grant you what you need now: suspension. Immunity. You are made of mist. This mistake is already forgiven."

When Curly gets to the boat he blinks. He sees her, blinks again—deliberately, she thinks, to clear his eyes and brain of the little apparition, the ghost of a boy who might have been his. And then he lunges.

He lunges for Toby with a long arm and misses, purposely. It's a beautiful leap. Curly is a poet whose medium isn't words. Toby has already gone with Curly along a trail where the witch is, in the dark and dangerous forests of the Brothers Grimm.

Toby isn't lost yet because he's left crumbs: that one little hand on Susan's thigh. But with his free hand, he takes a wild swing at Curly and they both laugh.

Curly dives into the barrel of net. He thrashes his arms and legs and pulls the apple green net, soft like moss, angel hair or old man's beard. He pulls and piles the net around him and is hidden and all hearts thump thump thump.

The lampposts along the waterfront have been as invisible as hydro wires on city streets, there but not there, and now, blink, the lamps fade up like house lights in a theatre, or like a dozen low moons in the sky.

Curly crawls out of the barrel, growling and grunting. His arms reach and grope for Toby. Toby's hand presses down hard on Susan's leg and he buries his face in her coat. Curly shudders, grabs and growls once more and collapses on the float. An act, Susan thinks, a performance, a poem.

Susan stands up and the two crewmen come to the side of the boat. She passes Toby into one guy's arms. The other gives Susan a hand on to the float. "Set him down," she says. "Thanks."

Curly makes a swipe at Toby's feet and Susan and Toby swerve out of reach.

There is that breeze that lifts the leaves, Susan thinks. Thank God for wind. She reaches for Toby's hand

and they climb the ramp which is steeper now because the tide is falling. She starts the car. There's no singing now. They bounce and bump around as she tries to avoid the deepest ruts in that parking lot.

Just as they reach the paved road, Toby turns to Susan. "Mum," he asks, "do you think I *could* go fishing with that man?"

Naming

This has been a strange week and it's only Friday. On Monday, Joe got a call from the bus station. They said there was a parcel for him. It was a box of records from an old friend who's switched to compact discs.

"Good buddy," Maury wrote, "Enjoy."

We have been meaning to bring one of the turntables up from the basement for a long time but the task keeps slipping to the bottom of our list. It would be such an enormous job to find any particular song amongst the thousands of albums down there. Instead, we sometimes mention a line or hum a fragment, and the memory or desire that accompanies the short form is acknowledged with a look. It is enough most of the time. The music is there, waiting for a time when there is more time and less noise.

There is so much noise in an ordinary day; so much to interfere with what the heart hears faintly.

"Good old Maury," Joe said.

He resisted Maury's friendship at first. "He's the

kinda guy who likes to sit around and drink coffee and talk about music," Joe said. "And I don't talk music," he said, "I play it."

The sound of baby Jessica down the well in Texas comes through into this room now. Jeremy's watching the video for the fifteenth time while he finds apples in the Crayola colouring contest. He must like knowing what happens next, knowing there is successful rescue.

I have the first sentence: "So much has happened this week..."

There is so much every week but sometimes, like this week, there seems to be a shape, a meaning, substance asking for a form. It is like flying over a group of islands and recognizing an archipelago. Or synchronicity. That sensation.

Julie calls me from the porch. Mommm!

Whaaatt!

I've silenced her, but now a sob's escaped.

I went to the porch and there she was scrunched in the corner shivering. "I am so cold," she said. "The wind turned my umbrella inside out and the handle broke too."

"It's almost time for karate," Jeremy said, recognizing his chance for attention. "You shrunk my ghi, but that's good, Mom. It was too big before. Where's Dad? If I'm late the instructor makes me do twenty-five pushups. My boots are too small. My plantar's wart isn't going away like the doctor said it would."

"Have you been wishing like she said?" I asked him.

"Sometimes," he said, "but sometimes I forget."

I ran bathwater for Julie. When she got out she came up behind me and said, "Lookit, now I'm warm."

She is dressed in layers of pj-type clothing. A pair of

her great-grandmother's long johns, a nightgown made by Nana, daughter of Great-gran, and topping that, a flannel shirt Nan bought at a garage sale. Nothing matches but it all does.

Spaghetti sauce simmers and Joe's come to ask if he should take the garlic bread out of the wrapper before he puts it in the oven.

"No. Yes. No."

So much has happened this week...

"Turn the oven to 400 but don't take the bread out of the foil. Don't put it in till the oven heats up."

They are hungry ahead of schedule.

"There's no spaghetti," Joe says.

I got up and found it.

We brought the turntable upstairs on Monday night and hooked it into an old reel-to-reel tape recorder for power. The albums are mint condition versions of what we have in the basement.

There is a full set of Emmylou, a full set of Bruce Springsteen, the *Copperhead Road* album. Lightfoot's *Don Quixote* album has a note on it: "This is a collector's record, Joe. Put it back in the sleeve."

One of the songs I've been longing for is on that Lightfoot album.

> She's a good old boat
> And she'll stay afloat
> Through the toughest gale and keep
>   smiling

Music filled the house. Monday, Tuesday, Wednesday.

But for one more day
She would like to stay
In the lee of Christian Island

No news. No current affairs.

On Wednesday night, I went to bed early with Don Delillo's novel, *Mao II*. It opens with the marriage of five thousand Moonies at Yankee Stadium. The panoramic view narrows to the parents of one bride. They search for her with binoculars.

I woke to words and music, to a phrase that, oddly, seemed to be the thought I'd gone to sleep with.

It sure feels stra-a-ange...

That fragment floated up the stairs. The words echoed what I'd felt last night before sleep. At first I thought that Joe had written a new song. Then I realized he was singing and strumming with a record. I drifted in and out of sleep and each time I woke the same phrase touched me.

It sure feels strange

In the morning, after the kids left for school, Joe said, "Come and listen to a song I found last night. There's a word I can't get."

Hey, I was famous in Missouri
Everybody knew my name...

"It's Tom T. Hall singing, but he didn't write it," Joe said. "Not too often he sings someone else's songs."

"It's not that often you get so set on learning a song," I said. "At first I thought you wrote it."

"I wish," he said. He set the needle down.

> Now it sure feels strange
> To be in South Dakota
> Out on the *Lannn*...

"What's that word?"

"Out on the land? Out on the lane?"

> Sometimes my heart feels heavy
> Sometimes my head feels light
> Sometimes I think back to Missouri
> Other times I feel all right.
> But it sure feels stra-a-ange...

"Maybe it's a crime connection. Maybe the word's 'arraign'."

"I thought of that," Joe said. "I've been singing anything that fits, anything that rhymes with *name*."

"But there's an expression. What is it? Where's the slang dictionary? 'On the lam'?"

On the run from the law, a fugitive.

The melody, the way Tom T., "the Storyteller," takes his time with a song, giving each line its own time—letting the validity of each emotion sink, settle or float—these things, and naming what it feels like to lose your name, give away your name, trade it in for another name that doesn't fit some days, feels like a lie—it was the combination Joe and I needed. We both felt the click, the opening.

It would have been enough, but later that morning as we listened to "the song" again and again, the phone rang. It was a woman from the School District office who'd been compiling a Native Studies curriculum. She asked me to read it. She didn't want editing so much as someone to read for "flow." There's a word for flow. Is it profluence? A forward movement.

If this woman told me to read the *History of the Peoples* before I read the *History of the Hudson Bay Fort*, it didn't register. The Hudson's Bay story was on top, so I read the stories backwards, frowning and full of questions. Had they decided to tell it this way so the students would raise the questions and later find the answers?

The first English ship to come to the Northwest was called *The Eagle*. The writer noted that the name "eagle" was "funny in a way." It was name and symbol for peoples in many lands, including the name of the clan of a great Tsimshian chief, Ligeex.

All day yesterday I puzzled over history—what's in and what's left out. I was curious about Ligeex, who married his daughter to a Hudson's Bay man. What about her story? When will it be told and by whom?

I set the manuscripts aside and finished my application for a diploma course in Adult Education. I'd been resisting the "Career Goal Statement," but it was simple enough: "This year I hit a brick wall with a group of students. I now think learning about learning is a responsibility not a choice."

"Put your cards on the table," my sister'd said when I asked for advice earlier in the term. "Lay it out," she said. "Tell the truth and you might be able to salvage something." She's been in the education business for a long time.

Two years ago Joe and I decided to get away for a weekend. We hadn't been away, alone together, for years. We'd just bought an '81 Rabbit, and we decided to drive to Prince George, five hundred miles from here, and spend the late November weekend. Shop, wine, dine and dance.

We stopped at Mountain Eagle in Smithers and I bought *Emotions*, a book by June Callwood, but it was too late to read once we got back on the road. Plus we had so much to say, all our wishes rolling out as we rolled along. There were hazards: black ice, a moose. There was a huge low moon.

We got into Prince George at midnight. It was ten below. In the morning, the car wouldn't start and we had to buy a new battery.

It wasn't only the car that went haywire that weekend. We bought too much, had too much to eat, too much to drink. When we got back to our room on Saturday night, I wanted to talk about excess and deprivation but Joe didn't. He had a smooth agate in his jacket pocket and he turned it over and over and over. When he passed it to me in place of words, I threw it at the mirror and it cracked.

We left early Sunday morning and for a long stretch of highway the cracks in the mirror seemed to be a terrible truth. There was nothing to say that wouldn't split us wide open.

I opened *Emotions*. Love, Hate, Fear and Other Lively Emotions, the cover said. "From the basic hates and fears of childhood to the more sophisticated feelings that later govern our lives." I cracked the spine. "Courage" was smack in the middle. Joe asked me to read to him as he drove.

"Courage is the quality humanity most admires,

though few people recognize it in themselves," I read. "The most remarkable heroism of which humans are capable is so quiet and seemingly ordinary that it is admired chiefly by the cognoscenti.

"Whoever they are," I said.

Joe was surprised I didn't know. "You're the one with all the words," he said.

"There are three areas of normal living which demand courage to be well met. One is marriage, one is social relations and the third is occupation.

"I want to be courageous," I said.

"Don't talk, read," Joe said.

"All growth, all change involves acts of courage. When people give up a prejudice or a long-held set of beliefs, they give up a piece of what they have been. It is wrenching and disturbing."

What is the long-held prejudice? That life should be easy? That life should flow? That there'll be no fear or regret, longing or nostalgia, no regret, no desire to escape? And what would be the name for that mixture of emotion between us that day as we travelled back down the Yellowhead Highway to the coast and our kids? Is it enough to recognize the emotion, to know that "it" is there?

Last night I began again. I started with fears I could name:

depths, esp. water
heights, esp. bridges

I get a dream over and over again that I am crossing one of those arched bridges. I am in the middle and I can't turn back and I can't go forward. I looked up *phobia* in the dictionary and discovered that there's a word for the fear of crossing bridges: gephroyophobia. Enough people experience this fear that it has been given a name.

There is a swinging bridge at Canyon City up the Nass Valley. If you want to go into that village, the bridge is the only way. It was windy the day I walked across that hammock strung between mountains over the green river. Kids played tag while I held on tight, inched my way along.

At midnight I picked up the Native Studies curriculum once more. I turned to the first section, titled "Northcoast Peoples and the Land." The text is part ada'ox', lessons written on the mind, passed from one generation to the next, and part explanation linking the stories. At the end of one chapter there was a list of names, examples of names individuals are given over the course of a life:

The Spray from the Fish's Fin is Like Eagle Down
The Eagle Sits Facing Seaward When Eating Its Food
Oolichan Stuck to the Ice on the Nass

Oolichan Stuck. I recognized my name, my fear. Not heights or depths really but being in the middle, held, unable to think my way out, off, up or down. Just stuck like an oolichan to the ice on the Nass, recalling past springs but incapable of believing another will come.

Last night while Joe was singing in the bar downtown, the rain that has fallen relentlessly all week stopped. The wind blew and the sound it made was like the sound the waves make. The wind in the cedars behind the house here was like the sound of waves washing on the shores of Lake Huron, my childhood home.

There must be layers of unidentified emotions in everyone and it's only when the wind blows a certain way that these feelings are stirred, uncovered, rediscovered.

I went to bed tired but all right.

At 4:30, Joe woke me up. He said he'd been home for a while but he couldn't sleep because of the wind.

"This warm dry wind doesn't blow very often," he said. "It would be too bad to miss it. Get up. You can sleep tomorrow."

He'd brought some old green coveralls upstairs for me. I put them on over my nightgown and made cups of tea spiked with dark rum and we stepped outside.

We have a large and wild backyard that borders on parkland. The Lawn Turns From Grass to Nettles and Salmonberry Bushes and To Cedars Seventy, One Hundred Feet High.

Joe had been sitting in one of the trees before he came to get me. He said:

The Tree Is a Natural Staircase
Don't Think About It, Just Climb
The Wind Blowing Through the Trees Is Like the
    Sound of the Waves on the Charlottes

We climbed high into the creaking arms of that tree. Each gust loosened nameless aches and fears and wishes.

"This is what we need," I said.

"Chinooks," he said.

"Yes," I said. "More Chinooks."

Say the Word

The boy is twelve and taller than Fran by several inches now. She has not seen much of him this summer since he is trolling with his uncle, away ten days at a time, in town for a day or two, then out, away again. Even when he is home, Fran hardly sees him because he sleeps until the phone rings or until one of the neighbourhood boys hollers up at his open bedroom window. Then he is in the bathroom, at the fridge, and before she can speak with him, out the door, skateboard under his arm.

He used to walk but now, just this summer, he has begun to glide. He is finding a stride that is a little like his father's way of navigating the world but not so sure or sturdy. The way the boy moves down the hall or down the road toward his friends is lighter than the way Joe walks. He seems to float as if he is several inches above the ground, and Fran wonders if time on the water has given him this ability.

The boy has just called from the fishing grounds and though they have said goodbye and hung up, Fran feels as if they are still connected—it's just a time of dead air, each waiting for the other to say something that might make a difference.

How are you, Fran asked him.

Good, he said, but his voice wasn't hearty.

Where are you. Yes, at Zayus, where the blackflies are not so bad as they are at Dundas, but where on the boat, where are you now? Below? In your bunk?

I'm in the wheelhouse. Where the phone is.

She'd heard a hint of sarcasm, a hint of what would come with his changing voice.

And where is Uncle Ronnie?

He's icing fish in the hold.

And was fishing good today?

I'm not going to make as much money as last trip. We're getting lots of humpies.

What else to ask him? What piece of news would give him pleasure, something to mull over?

You got a skateboard catalogue in the mail today.

What's on the cover?

Oh, Jer, she'd said, I don't know if I can find it in this mess. We're still sanding the floors, you know. We're upside down.

Will you try, he'd asked.

Okay. Hold on, she'd said, rummaging through a pile of papers on the table. Jackpot, Jer. You're lucky. It's a dark blue, a nighttime sky and there's tall white buildings, like towers or highrises, and a big steep ramp.

You mean a half-pipe?

I don't know what it is. It's this big curved thing that's joined up to the buildings and there's a boy hanging in the air on his skateboard. He's just come off the ramp and the photographer took a picture of him hanging there in the sky.

What's on the second page?

She'd laughed, flipped the page, and told him a little about the advertising for "completes," tops, trucks, wheels and bearings and then said maybe they'd talked enough for one night. It was good Uncle Ronnie bought that new phone that reached from the grounds to home, wasn't it? Was there anything else he wanted to say?

Will you put the catalogue on my bed?

That's it? That's all? She'd encouraged him to say a little more. After all, they had privacy. Not like on a radio-phone where every word you said crackled in the galleys of all the boats on the grounds.

Well, there's *something* else.

And what is that?

I'm afraid I'm going to drown. I'm afraid I'm not going to come home from this trip.

And Fran had said, Of course you will. Do you think we'd let you go fishing if we were even a little bit worried about you? But at the same time she saw the wall at the waterfront park, built with bricks, hundreds of bricks bearing the names of those who were lost at sea, life spans both long and short. Fran wishes Joe had been home. His words might a difference. What he'd say might help the boy get through it.

Fran stood inside the doorway of the boy's room, looking at the things that represented his spirit at twelve. He collected far less junk than any of them, discarded his past passions and dreams easily and often. Ninja Turtles and that pair of nunchucks he'd ordered from the back of a comic for 19.95 US dollars: two heavy-duty plastic sticks attached with a chain arrived in a cardboard tube. A weapon. Where would he swing those sticks? At whom? Did they work like a boomerang? Did you swing them and let go? The boy had looked surprised. Enemies? Robbers, maybe. Killers.

Pirate ship and space station Lego sets were long gone. Now his walls were plastered with posters of Pavel and Linden but these were tattered and droopy because the pins and staples had fallen out. They were ready for the garbage. She knew what posters came next: Smashing Pumpkins, Kurt Cobain, Hendrix, Rage Against the Machine.

She got clean sheets, made his bed and flapped the quilt his gran had made for him from old wool coats that had belonged to the men in the family. She watched the quilt float down and settle, smoothed out the wrinkles and sat down facing his CD player. Last summer's fishing had bought it. This icon. The machine and the neatly piled discs held his deepest self, his hopes, fears, dreams. The machine, the music, the shelf: an altar.

Above the CD shelf, he'd hung an 8x10 picture of himself in a deep blue hand-knit sweater and leggings set. The photograph had been taken in Woolworth's on his first birthday. Fran had carried him partway through the store and then set him down, held his hand while he took head-first topple-over steps. What a beautiful boy, the grandmothers in the store had said that December day. What a beautiful boy.

Beside the portrait was a newspaper clipping of his gran and grampa taken fifty years ago on their wedding day, their heads touching, tilted in toward each other, their eyes startling in their shiny innocence. These three faces had held their places throughout the boy's changes, but this year, Fran thought, he'll take them down from the wall and put them in a shoebox. Of course he has to do this.

Fran reached behind her and turned out the light. The glow-in-the-dark stars on the boy's ceiling were dim from where she sat and she wondered if they shone brighter when Jer lay down, thinking of the faraway future, or if they shone bright just for the next day and were faint and misty, ghostly even, when he thought of the years ahead. Did he imagine what it would be like if she died, if his father died, where he would go, what he would do? She lay down on the single bed with the skateboard magazine across her breasts.

By now he would be in his narrow upper bunk, inside his blue sleeping bag. He would have warmed his hands on the engine pipes after some last chore on deck. He'd have brushed his teeth in the tiny sink, gotten rid of the taste of diesel fuel for a moment, then turned out the light, crawled up, opened the tiny porthole and cranked his neck around so he could see the black water and the dark grey rainy skies. No stars, no dipper, no moon.

And what would he think? Would he take his mind directly to the skateboard catalogue, remember that she'd promised to put it on his bed, or would he have to take the long way to that thought, first listening to the waves elapsing like slow seconds on the sides of the wooden boat, then thinking of falling over the side, how it might happen to him the way it had happened to others. He would try not to think about the men floating in the water with their zippers open, but these dead men would knock and bump and nudge the sides of the boat. He would spend some time hating his dad for telling him about it, for making him show him how he could plant his feet solid, two feet apart, one a little ahead, think about how he hated being given a push, a playful but hard and sudden push which toppled him and proved that he wasn't planted, didn't have his feet or his mind solid or determined, didn't have sea legs yet.

And boots. New yellow and black Helly Hansons, size 11, the same size as his dad's and his uncle's. Last year just regular gumboots from the back of Zellers, $15.99, and now these new ones, $60 off his crew share. Buying them with his uncle in Fisherman's Supply. He's getting in deeper and deeper. And he never asked for it, except he did ask if he could fish again this summer. For the money. Now he has his own rain gear and six pairs of black gloves and a scar from when one of the hooks flew through the flesh below his thumb. Six pinpoint needle marks from the barbs on a cod. How weird and numb his whole arm went. He would think about crab bait, fish heads, his head, and then about his hand with the two big warts that won't go away even though the doctor dropped stuff on them twice this summer.

His father and uncle had made him practise kicking his boots off. Faster, they yelled at him. See how fast you can get them off. You gotta kick hard. And even a survival suit now. For him. Uncle Ron said it was for the boat, but then why did he have to try it on in his living room. Lay it out like it's your shadow and get in as fast as you can, his dad said.

The fisherman who drowned just before they'd left on this trip. He fell off the dock, slipped or something coming down the ramp, boards greasy with rain and oil, and fell into the harbour right beside his own boat and no one was there to help him.

What would it be to lose him? Fran panicked, feeling as though she had fallen in herself. She kicked away from those thoughts. Did she think she could travel with the boy all his life, be his life ring? No. But she imagined she could go a long distance with him, maybe all her life, all of his, if she just floated. His dreamy way invited this kind of quiet companionship, knowing, didn't it?

This boy. He didn't use words. It wasn't his way. When he was nine, they'd been doing dishes together. He was washing. The radio was tuned into the local pop station, low, part of the air. And the air between them was easy as it mysteriously always has been—a live and let live. Lots of space and air, a sink full of water and suds. The boy liked the dishes to be clean. He didn't hurry. And she didn't say c'mon c'mon, speed it up, get the job done. He had pushed his hand and the dish cloth into a glass and let it fill up with water. After a bit of turning and swishing he'd held the glass up for her. His fist was crammed against the side and his thumb and finger made a kind of sad dreamy smile.

This is how I'd look if I drowned, he said.

He'd been swimming in the town pool earlier that week, he told her. The words came slowly. She'd pumped and pressed them out of him, a few at a time, as they carried on washing and drying. Shane, that bully, had held him under in the deep end. Jer dried his hands, pulled the neck of his tee shirt down onto his shoulder, and she saw the bruises on his back, his collarbone, faint blue fingerprints. She loathed that boy Shane, but kept drying and setting the dishes in the cupboard. He had struggled but Shane had held him down harder so he stopped fighting and waited.

After that watery revelation, she and Joe began to preach. You've got to get mad. Say no. Say to yourself: I will not sink. I will not go under. This will not happen to me. Find that place in your head, Fran had said. No, said Joe, find that place in your body.

Had any of these words sunk into his skin? Or did they drift through him, in one ear and out the other?

Words. He doesn't use them but Fran has noticed how the boy is drawn and held by the way she and his sister talk sometimes, as if he is warming his hands at a fire. He comes in close but he rarely adds wood. Perhaps he knows that the beach has been combed and that there is enough on the fire to keep it burning without his help. This thought makes Fran sad. How can you survive without words to keep you warm when you are shivering with cold after falling in? Still, lately, when the four of them gathered by chance at the kitchen table, a girl and a boy, a man and a woman, they'd built some rip-roaring fires and the laughter had leapt like cinders between them.

Before the boy left on this trip, there'd been a flareup between Joe and Julie, some normal thing like Julie used all the hot water when Joe needed to have a shower too. Normal and then escalated, Julie storming upstairs to her room and Joe retreating to his basement quarters. That left Fran and Jer on the middle deck. Jer headed for the television in the front room and Fran turned on the radio in the kitchen and began to wash dishes. Vicki Gabereau was live on the Fraser River, rushing down through white water. Her squeals of fear and exhilaration rose and fell in Fran. She dried her hands on the tea towel and went to check on Jer. He was lying on the couch watching *Dumb and Dumber*, hands cupped behind his head. He paused the movie with the remote.

Do you feel sad or anything, he'd asked.

No, she'd said. And they had gazed at each other, amused, amazed. They had floated through the storm untouched, dry as a bone.

Yes, what she knows of him so far is his calm floating soul. If you don't tell me things, she'd said to him recently, I just think, Oh, Jer—his life is perfect. He'd looked at her as if she were insane. Not long ago, when the four of them were together at breakfast, Jer said he'd had a dream about falling down a deep hole and the more he tried to climb out the deeper the hole grew. And then somebody mentioned a jogger, how his wife had said he ran in his sleep and the sheets and blankets got all whipped up. Joe had talked of flying. How joyous to look at the stick-on stars and think of him soaring over Grassy Lake, flying high and tilting down into the cove where Duffy has set up his bachelor camp, watchman at the dam. Fran soared too, circled. She saw two teenage boys, a case of beer, a canoe, a moon. The boys were laughing and then the canoe, the canoe tipped and the boys strug- gled in the icy water, laughing at first and grasping for the boat. Laughing and then gasping, unable to believe what was happening.

This country has become treacherous now, Fran thought. Before kids, she'd decided that to think too much about what might happen would be to invite disas- ter. If your number was up, it was up. Still, on the sea- planes crossing the Hecate Straits in storms, she'd made deals with God. I'll do this if you will do this. The engine stalled on a plane Joe was on. He didn't mention any deals. He said he put his duffel bag in front of his face and chest, thinking it might cushion the blow when it came.

And the Skeena River. Every year, sometimes twice a year, someone, sometimes families, slid in. Old cars, brand new cars, four-wheel-drive all-terrainers, logging trucks. And lives, swallowed whole by this huge grey whale. If it wasn't the river side of the highway, it was the mountains that slid down once a year, twice a year, caving in on travellers whether they were making business deals or going to a hockey tournament with all intentions of bringing home a trophy for the town.

Now any story of survival, of how people kept their wits about them, seems important to repeat, to discuss.

Last year at the end of the summer, two boys had left their village in a canoe. They packed for an overnight adventure, intending to paddle to the far side of an island and set up camp. Their canoe tipped in the breakers as they approached what they thought was the spot they wanted and though they made it to shore, they weren't found for three days. Their grandfather, who was aboard the rescue boat, told the crew where the boys would be and there they were, wet, cold and hungry. "You went the wrong way," the grandfather said. "Well, why didn't you tell us?" the boys said. "You watched us leave. You heard us planning. Why didn't you tell us?"

"You didn't ask," said the grampa.

Fran keeps remembering this story and telling it to her kids. Now after what happened to them, the boys *will* ask, she says. *Wanting* to know is so much better than being *told* what you should know, she says to them. But she wonders: How did the grandfather keep his mouth shut? Where did he find his trust? How could he risk so much?

Fran wonders if Jeremy remembers the fire lesson, the day they went out for blueberries, filling an ice cream bucket along the tracks, and then climbing higher onto the rock bluffs above the harbour, scrambling on those cliffs. They found a sheltered place to rest, and the kids had said, Let's make a fire. Okay, said Joe. But you only have one match. Pretend you are lost and you only have one match. How would you make the best of your one chance? The kids had the right instinct—they'd gathered small twigs and propped them up like a teepee—but the match didn't catch. Look under the trees, go into the bush a little, look for the driest finest smallest burnable things. Dry brown needles, anything like that. The wind off the water was really cold when the sun disappeared. Did Jer remember that time on the bluff? Would he remember it if he needed it?

What would it be to lose him? Could she hold on to the story, the making lost into found, that the singer for the Haida dancers had explained before the dancers danced the story in their red and black, this life and that other one? How all the village mourned as they searched for a little lost girl, how in spring, they saw the first salmon jump in the creek, joyful, and they knew it was their little girl, come back to them. She had heard parents say that after a while, after the passing of several seasons, they saw their lost children appear in spring, not in a fish, perhaps, but in a flower, the first purple crocus raising its head through the snow.

Every mother and father goes to the place in them where the child is lost. If they do not imagine it, fall into it through events around them, through a neighbour, a friend, a relative, then it happens through the news, the falling into that empty unimaginable pit. And if they refuse to fall in waking life, then the descent comes in dream. The child about to fall from a cliff, drown in the lake, be murdered by ... and the hopeless grasping, stretching out to reach the hand of the child, kicking, swimming toward him, never getting there, the sheets and blankets churning. Nobody speaks of these dream deaths. Fran has never told hers to anyone but Joe, and even then, she left out details and went straight for the interpretation—"worry," a need making itself known through dream to make sure the boy, the girl, had survival skills.

The boy will come home. What is happening to him now is natural and good and at twelve he must walk through it on his own. He has to learn to manage fear—waking and sleeping—to fear in dreams and wake from them, to fear before sleep, and in all the long days on the water. He needs to remember and invent survival, to imagine himself as eagle, otter, boy in a canoe paddling to an island for a weekend adventure.

She can't do anything but wave goodbye, go with him in spirit. He will walk through it, glide through the door as he has done at the end of every trip this summer. She knows he can and will. He must. She rises, smooths the bed, and lays the magazine on his pillow.

That new boat phone. The cellular. Did it help or hinder the walking through?

Did you tell Uncle Ron you were afraid of drowning? she'd asked.

Yes, he said. I have a whistle around my neck.

Facing the Altar

Dear Belle and Eileen,

Eileen, you phoned at such a good time today. The kids had gone down to the docks with their fishing poles, a little package of last year's frozen halibut for bait, and a pearl-handled jackknife to cut it. I mention the jackknife because it was part of an offering Mom made to Jeremy last time we were home. "I have a few things gathered for you," she said to him one night when he was a little bored, and she disappeared down the basement stairs and was back up quick as a wink. She set an old tin lunch kit of mine on the table. "Is there anything in this for *you*?" she asked Jer, inviting him to pick through odds and ends she had collected—an old hand drill, a stump of a carpenter's pencil, a handmade chisel and a small hammer like the kind you might use for upholstering. Naturally, Jer chose the jackknife. I asked for the lunch kit because it brought Dad's grin back to me so clearly the second I saw it. He'd found a smooth strip of metal to replace the broken handles and bolted the new strip on to the box. I cried because it looked so ugly and refused to take it to school. Sigh. Who fixes lunch kits any more? Who saves them for thirty-five years to give to a grandson? Anyway, Eileen, you put the heat on. It was time to make the decision. Yes or no. I've known all along that we couldn't afford to fly home for Mom's birthday, but I guess I thought we might win the lottery or something.

And Belle, thanks for your call an hour ago with the idea to send a tape with our family's tributes to Mom. Eighty years old! A tape. Simple, no problem. A great idea. I thought I could get it in the mail tonight, but I can't get started without more talk with the two of you. I need more warmup before the official version. Like I said, it makes me homesick to think of the village—our village— the farmhouse and everyone gathered there, the two of you driving up to the country from your separate cities a day or two early to get in some real talk and real time together.

I can see your white and silver cars parked side by side on the gangway to the barn. The old mother cat and her newest kittens, shy and skittery, will come down from the hay mow, and mew for scraps and milk. The two of you will be making salads, desserts, lasagnas, arranging bouquets of sweetpeas for the harvest table, designing a banner to stretch from one end of the front room to the other. Is it homesickness or yearning? A feeling of being just out of earshot when important things are being said. I am listening right now for your voices, can almost hear what you are saying, will say, enough to put two and two together the way I used to when I listened in the stairwell to the conversations you two had with Mom or Dad after I'd been sent up to bed.

Julie just came to say goodnight—a kiss and a glance at all the paper I've crumpled up. "Is it hard to write to Aunt Eileen and Aunt Belle in the same letter?" she asked. I told her it was going to be easy, that writing about her gramma, a kind of speech for everybody to hear, would be the hard thing. "Could I read the *letter*?" she asked. I said "Probably," and she went up to bed. So. Where were we? At the kitchen table in your summer house, Belle, but now there's another dimension. It's as if Julie is above us looking down through the ornate iron register in the hall.

She comes to me more and more often these days to talk. She lingers, dawdles, until Jer has brushed his teeth and headed upstairs, and then she begins. She has a way of phrasing things—simply, but with a depth and a gentleness—always opening with a question that intrigues me.

For instance: Mom, can you help who you fall in love with? I asked her why she was thinking about that. She took a long route through a book she'd been reading about a girl who fell in love with someone else's boyfriend. She said she liked both girls and she liked the guy too and so she didn't know how to feel. If you *could* stop yourself, then she *would* know how to feel.

I said I didn't think you could decide about love but I thought you could decide how to act. Doesn't that sound like an answer Mom would give?

And another night: If someone asked you to write down the most important things in your life, would you like that? I said it would depend on who asked me. It turned out her teacher had given her class forty-five minutes to answer a series of questions which Julie didn't want to answer. He kept telling them they had to answer honestly, that they couldn't skip a question. She said she was the last to finish. Her friend Willow was swearing and Angie was crying. She wished she hadn't written some things. "There's things I wouldn't tell you," she said.

She surprises me all the time now and she's only eleven. This mother/daughter relationship, the one they write all the books about, is a mystery that's never solved, isn't it? It's boggling how deep the bond is. Love and guilt. Even to speak of the bond, to try to get to it, feels like betrayal, doesn't it? The two of you with your grown daughters, how much do you think your relationship echoes, imitates the closeness and distance you had with Mom? How much a reaction against it? I wish I could be there for your stories.

Belle, that summer you came home with your kids to help Mom and Dad in the store when Dad was getting so weak, was the summer of my first boyfriend, Jake. You've probably forgotten all about that. One Sunday Mom made one of her memorable brunches, side and back bacon, eggs fried in the drippings, two kinds of cheddar cut from the round blocks in the hinged glass case in the store, bread from the little inland bakery, and two kinds of homemade jam, strawberry and peach. After we ate, you and I and Mom cleared the table, getting ready to do the dishes. I had been out with Jake the night before at the drive-in and later on a back road near the lake, and my lips were tender and bruised. I was fifteen. "I'm in love," I announced. "I'm in love and love making love go together." Mom gasped before she turned her back.

I wanted her to argue with me, to give me some good reasons, to convince me that sex at fifteen was outside the bounds of what she could tolerate. But in retrospect, I see how effective the gasp was. I'd hurt her. Shocked her. Mission accomplished. Mission accomplished on her side too. I didn't act for a few more years. One gasp for breath on her part gave me some breathing time.

She's never argued with me. She listens to me argue with myself. Her head goes down and she waits it out. She is an ear, a receiver, a reflector, a deflector, a mirror. When I complain sometimes about how hard marriage is, call long distance on a black day, desperate for a word or two of acknowledgement about how unfair, unmovable, un/dis/etc. my husband is, she will not satisfy me. Will not discuss his flaws. All she'll say is: You can't change the other fella.

Once I asked Mom if she was close to her mom and she said, "Too close." She wouldn't go further. She dismissed my questions with a wave of her hand.

Do you think she felt every nuance of her mother's life, from the time she was a child in that family of twelve, getting an orange, a pencil and a new pair of lace-up boots for Christmas? Knowing Mom, she probably suffered what her mother suffered, was filled with gladness when her mother was filled. But when do you think she realized what it meant? When did she put the words "too close" to it?

Did Mom ever answer your questions about Aunt Charlotte? When I asked Mom how her mother could give a child to someone else to raise, Detroit so far away in those days of the Model T or whatever, she answered without hesitation. "It wasn't 'someone,' it was a sister. They had the same ways about them, the same values." I tried to get a little more info. Why did Aunt Charlotte have such a nervous temperament? Why did she die so young? "Life," Mom said. "Life hits people differently." No more words on that topic. So many things resting in the vault that is our mom, eh? Not locked, exactly, but in repose, respectfully wrapped in tissue, waiting for the right time, the right person.

Whoa! This is getting heavy. I'd better get moving. Just one little story that relates to Mom's offerings. I guess I've had it wrapped in tissue—stored—for the right time to unwrap it again, admire it for its place in the history of mother/daughter relationships. This happened the night before Joe and I got married.

"You were seventeen when you got married, right?" I said to Mom.

"And three-quarters," she said with a quick look to Joe.

We were sitting around after dinner going over our lists—we each had a system for keeping track of jobs that had to be done before seven the next day. I had a cloth diary, Joe had a day-planner and Mom used old envelopes which she kept together with an elastic band, current day on top. I was going to pick up the flowers and call the pipers to ask them to come to the dinner as well as to the church. Dave was going to go to the liquor store. Mom was concerned, at this last minute, that we needed to have a midnight lunch. Should we have trays made up at the deli or should we buy the meats, cheeses and crackers and fix trays at home when the two of you arrived in the morning ready to roll up your sleeves?

"And three-quarters..." I gave her a prompt, hoping she'd tell us a little about her courtship. "For Joe's sake," I said. She bowed her head for minute and came up smiling with the few words, the summary. How she met Dad at the country inn and dance hall his parents owned early in the century, how her older brothers played fiddle regularly, how they'd asked Mom to chord for them that night. "How old was Dad?" I asked. She looked first at me and then at Joe. "Twenty-nine." "And did he take you home that night?" I asked. "Yes," she said, hesitating for a moment. "In the horse and buggy." "And did he kiss you?" "That's enough," Mom said. She made a dot, a period on her envelope. We laughed. She circled the dot, enlarged it.

We had been staying with her for a week, sleeping together in the basement bedroom, that one I had when Mom and I first moved to town after Dad died. We'd flown in from the coast and Mom met us at the airport. I had that gorgeous white wool coat on, Eileen, the one you lent me the money to buy, thank you, yards of soft cloth falling from the shoulder. Mom wouldn't say, "Well, let's have a look." Not at the airport, not in front of Joe. I knew she wouldn't. But the first minute we were alone, I asked her to come downstairs to look at my dress. She said, "It's certainly the right choice."

I wanted to ask her, "How pregnant do I look?" but I couldn't. Instead I asked, "You're still okay? The church? The aisle? All the old country neighbours?" You remember, I hadn't realized till all the arrangements were made that I'd be five months along, not three. She gave me a long, penetrating look and then she said: Pregnancy has nothing to do with facing the altar.

I was thirty. That's ten years older than either of you when you married and what, twelve and one-quarter years older than Mom? She married in the '20s. Belle, you married the year after I was born, and Eileen, I remember being so excited about going to your wedding. 1964. Mom and I went to the Fashion Shoppe to get dresses to wear to it. Mom bought a navy linen and I got a navy one with white polka dots on the ruffles around the neck and down the front, the new Piccadilly style.

Mom and Dad and I drove to Toronto for your wedding. We were late for the ceremony. They didn't want to go to the church because you were marrying a Catholic, turning. They liked Martin but they didn't like the heavy hand of that church. Dad had a flask of whiskey in the glove box. He took a swig and put the flask in the inside pocket of his suit.

Once I asked Mom about the drinking in Dad's family. "Your dad could take it or leave it," she said. "I always liked him when he'd had a drink. It just made him a little more of what he already was."

When Dad died the next year, I'd just broken up with Jake, that first boyfriend, and he came to the wake with his father and all his brothers. They were so handsome, that whole family of Catholics.

I wish I were there with you! If we were together now, I know we'd be laughing. I just have to stop for a minute and I can hear it.

One night Jake talked about us getting married. I was only in grade ten. Jake said I should finish grade twelve and go to teachers' college for a year. His older brother had married a teacher and it was good for a farmer to be married to someone with a steady income. He said, "You'd have to turn Catholic but your dad won't mind." I don't think I answered for a minute or two. I remember feeling a *ping* like when you're driving on a gravel road and a stone hits the windshield and makes a mark but doesn't shatter the glass. Jake hadn't included Mom in his assessment of what support we might need or what hurdles we'd have to jump. In any case, I was all for becoming Catholic because I loved their big red brick church with the spire that you could see from a mile away, and their garden parties on the church lawn, lanterns lit after sunset. And the people—the variety—they seemed so much more fun than us Presbyterians. They could do what they wanted and then confess and start over. I was more than ready to be Catholic, it was the grade twelve and then teachers' college part that rang the alarm in my head.

Belle, there's that one picture of you in your wedding suit. Was it navy? You're wearing a little hat with a jaunty feather and I am sitting in a chipped porcelain washtub at the back of the house where the wood was weathered. That must have been the day you and John left for Maine and then for Germany and the air force. After Germany, whenever you came home to visit, you and John slept in that room papered with pink roses.

I used to move from room to room but my favourite was your old room, Eileen, where you climbed out on the roof over the kitchen to sun tan. I wanted to do everything you did. Remember those pictures of you and Teresa and Lizzy in rolled-up blue jeans and bobby socks posing out there, like pinup girls, holding the only house cat we ever had? I remember your Black Cat cigarettes, Belle.

When you and John were home I loved hearing the two of you talk and talk and talk when you came upstairs to bed. I couldn't hear what you said but I could hear the back and forth of it and sometimes laughter. I wanted a marriage exactly like yours, Belle. I wanted to lie in bed and smoke a cigarette and talk, and the man I married was going to put his arm around my shoulders just like John had his around yours.

I didn't want to leave that house and the store and the village. I hated that town they call the prettiest little one in Canada. I hated Mom for selling our world and moving us into that tidy little red brick bungalow on the tidy maple-lined streets and I raged at her. Mom must have mourned for Dad, for herself, for all that was lost, but I never saw a tear.

I used to call her an old nun. I said, "You don't laugh, you don't cry, you don't feel anything. You're just an old nun." Why didn't she slap my face? She had an expression that drove me crazy: Sorry did nothing.

Julie's only eleven but she can nail me with words already. And I rise to it. I nail her right back. And only then, after the words are out, do I remember Mom's technique: No answer. Turn cheek. I said, "You're stingy. You won't give me anything about what you feel. You won't give me anything." Julie's just starting to say, "You're stupid. You're so stupid."

That night before the wedding, I asked Joe if he'd mind sleeping in the hotel. I wanted to be alone with Mom. His folks had come into town that day and though he didn't say it, I think he wanted their imprint on him. He borrowed Mom's car for the night but before he left we stood in the driveway watching the falling snow turn everything white. It was so soft and we were so strong and sure.

When I came back inside, into the kitchen, Mom's face was changed somehow, more alive, alert, open. "Now," she said, with a look and a smile. "Now," she said again, "I have to wash and set my hair. Bear with me while I do this little job and then we'll get to the important things." She didn't want to go to the hairdresser's with me in the morning, didn't want to take time for it. "These hours are precious," she said. She draped her blouse and cardigan around the back of her chair. She stripped down to the full slip and slim skirt with a kick-pleat. You know those slips, she must have four or five of them, forty years old, white and silky, always hand-washed and hung to dry on the line. She wipes the line with a clean soft rag before she hangs anything, even a rug.

I am thinking now of two more expressions of hers:

Absolute attention is prayer
Do the little things

The last time I was home she remembered that Joe's grandma liked poppies but had only red ones. Gran's poppies looked so beautiful in that mess of wild green where she lived in her crooked clapboard house. Mom had dusky pink poppies along her back fence and she picked off the seed pods, broke the seeds into an old salt shaker and put a bit of waxed paper inside the lid so the seeds wouldn't spill out till they got to Gran's garden.

I used to think Gran was so opposite to Mom because Gran talked constantly. But since her death, stories about her life have come down from the attic and I'm finding out how much she buried. I understand now that her talk was always of today, of the business of the day. She cut off questions about her past. "Guilt is a useless emotion," Gran used to say.

Mom and Gran, the same generation. They were taught the same things, that there were things you didn't say, stories you didn't tell. They accepted silence, swallowed their particular struggles, while struggling to find universal truths to express them.

Mom's slip straps kept sliding off her shoulders down onto her thin muscled arms. You know how she likes to say she wears size seven, not five. "Seven sounds a little better," she says. I was drinking tea, watching her, absorbing her. I'd offered to help with her hair but she said no, she had a good system worked out. Twice I got up to slide the straps back on to her shoulders.

She said, "I think it's ten minutes for this rinse," as she shook the drops of Clairol Silver Highlite into her palms, her back curled over the sink. "Check it for me, Chickadee." Those words—and her tone—so breathy and affectionate—that was the gift I received. Her rush of unchecked feeling, no weighing of words, no weight on them as they flew out of her.

"Now," she said. "Now."

She had already gathered all her hair-styling equipment and set it out on the table. The antique swivel mirror, the cardboard Eddie Bauer skate box filled with rollers—sponge, brush, mesh, plastic, clamps, picks, nets and pages torn from magazines—before-and-after articles, the set shown, little arrows indicating the direction to roll.

I asked her if she'd like me to do the set. She said she'd like a cup of tea. I began to talk about the baby, asking her if she'd come west when it was born. "Save that subject for a day or two," she said.

When she finished rolling she wrapped a net around her head. She put away the gear and filled her cup with hot water from the kettle. "Now," she said again. Bright. Quick.

Up she went in her low-heeled suede pumps, up the stairs to her bedroom with the sharply sloped ceiling and her carved mahogany bed, the green velvet settee, that clock Dad got for her—iron with a light spray of gold, cherubs carved around the face.

I followed her, stood in the doorway looking in. The white chenille spread, four pillows. That huge mahogany dresser, its deep, long drawers. When we lived in the village, when I was ten or twelve, I used to go into Mom and Dad's bedroom when they were in the store. I found tampax, brassieres, girdles, tried all. I found a black pouch and I didn't know what was in it.

Julie digs into my drawers, helps herself to my clothes—which are too big for her but she sneaks out with them, wears them anyway, my sweaters, tee shirts. My best earrings are missing but she denies taking them. Once she came to me in a sheer shorty nightshirt I hadn't even worn yet. I'd been saving it for sometime when the kids were away. When I saw her in it I felt like I'd been shot.

Mom sat on the edge of the bed. I went to her dresser as I'd always done when we were in that house in town and began opening drawers. It was a ritual now, not a secret one, but a way of talking with her, picking out one thing or another, asking about it, getting a little more story each time. I started with the top drawers, with the letters she stores in a cigar box. In this same box, she had saved x-rays of my teeth in the original late 1950s orthodontist's envelope. She had written "Fran" in ballpoint pen, underlined it twice. I asked her why she still had them.

"The way you were," she said, far away for an instant, the phone ringing in the middle of the night, a policeman at her door. Then back into this world, this room that held her most private self. "Toss them," she said, gesturing to the wastebasket. "Close that drawer. Try the middle one."

You know how beautiful her teeth are, a bit yellow but straight and how she sometimes flashes that shy wide smile? When she said, "Try the middle one," she had that same smile that's in her wedding picture. There was an old box in that drawer, a pretty one from Himmelhocks, a Detroit department store. "Bring that box out," she said.

I sat down on the bed, set the box between us and lifted the lid. Inside, under layers of tissue, a black silk negligee with black lace insets on the breast cups, string straps. It was not new. There were no tags. Not size fifteen but seven, the seven she was at seventeen.

"Try it on," she said as quick and light as she'd said Chickadee. "Try it on," she said, "and let me have a look."

The end. The end of this letter, anyway. I don't think I'm any closer to making a tape for the dinner celebration than I was a couple of hours ago. I might just send a tape directly to Mom. I'll call her, tell her I'm working on it. She'll understand.

Lotsa love,
Fran

Mean

Before Maura and Ben came to our school I never really thought about what it means to be mean. Before Maura and Ben, the Gerrards were the only kids we were sometimes mean to but they were always mean to us first. Especially Doraleen. I am not mean to her. It's just that I'm scared that if I'm too nice to her she'll sit beside me at lunch and give me one of her brown sugar sandwiches. I know I couldn't swallow it and that would be mean if you couldn't eat someone's food that they gave you.

We are not mean, we just try not to look at her. She tears off a piece of her sandwich and she licks off the sugar and she talks at us with her mouth open and little gobs spray out. We don't want to get too close to the Gerrards. Except I kind of like Tom Gerrard and I do like Freddie. There used to be Raymond but he was expelled, and there's more kids at their house down the side road. It's made of cement like a jail and I try not to stare at it when we go by in the school bus which is a station wagon with wood along the sides of it. The Gerrards don't come in our bus load from the village. The bus driver makes three loads every morning and three loads every night. If you get picked up last in the morning you go home first at night. So it's fair. It's four miles to our school and there are twenty-nine kids altogether in the eight grades. Our store is on the highway and then there's five houses in our village. All along the highway and up the side roads are houses and barns and silos and steers and cows. The McTavishes have a bull. Most kids have to walk out long lanes to wait for the bus, but I can stand in the store and see the bus coming down the road. I am lucky.

On our bus ride we go by the Gerrards' house. Sometimes I don't want to look at it because it makes me feel funny. Their dad comes to our store but not very often. He is grey and square like his house. If he brings one of his boys with him, he tells him to pump the gas and his words sound like he is throwing something that they'd better duck from. If he buys them a treat, he throws it at them and they have to move quick to catch it and I don't like to watch.

My dad is the same size as Morris Gerrard but his hair is white, not grey, and if I am sad he kind of teases me a little bit at a time until I feel better. The only time I don't like him is when I'm in the store and he says to Dad that I must be eating too much candy. My dad always says, "We're going to ship her out for baby beef." I guess he has to say something back but I wish he'd just walk away. He fell down last week and I found him out where we empty the ashes and the slop pail that we keep in the back kitchen. He couldn't talk or get up. I ran to the store to get Mom and she said to go and get Sarah's dad from his field that's behind our house and store. Him and Mom got Dad to the couch in the kitchen and then the doctor came from town in a convertible with the top down. The doctor likes my dad. He has a cottage at our beach and we see him in his shorts in the summertime. Dad has something wrong in his middle ear that made him fall down.

I like to be near him after I play my woodshed game, especially in the winter. This game is I am poor and I have to find food and make warm beds for my babies. Sometimes I am a field mouse and sometimes I am sort of like the Virgin Mary. In the summer there's the garden and blackcurrants and gooseberries and minnows to catch in the creek. In winter it's hard. We are hungry and cold. I sweep sawdust and the chips from the woodshed floor and the earth floor looks nice and clean but it is so cold and dark. The snow drifts outside the open doorway and swirls and I can't see my real house any more. And then I get scared of my game and go into our house, which is empty and dark but warm. I take off my mittens and shake the ice balls on to the stove top and they bounce and sizzle. I make some toast and then go to the store. I sit on a stool behind the counter and read a book or draw pictures of girls with pony tails and turned-up noses, their heads turned sideways, the way my sister taught me how to do it. She is in college now. We used to fight but I miss her. My brother is grown up and married and he lives in town with his wife, Kaila, and their two kids. I am an aunt and I'm only ten. It's good when they all come home and all the bedrooms in the house are full. I am lonesome almost all the time, but I have friends, too.

All the farmers come to the store at night after they finish their chores and they sit by the stove at the back of the store where we have things like caps and shirts and rubber boots and teacups and birthday cards. They sit on nail kegs or wooden pop crates and smoke and talk about things that happened that day or a long time ago. My dad doesn't talk that much but he adds things at the ends of stories and the men laugh. My friend Sarah's dad and my dad sometimes say funny things to each other for a long time, back and forth.

Morris Gerrard doesn't sit at the back of the store. He pays cash for the things he buys. When I am in the store alone I flip through a filing cabinet in the post office. The cabinet is like a big cash register, or like a big dictionary with tin pages. Everybody who lives around here has bills and they are held down on the tin pages with springy things like mousetraps or wire clothespins. Morris Gerrard's spring is stretched out wide. He's not allowed to charge anything else until he pays his old bills. I'm not supposed to know this but I do. Once I asked my dad if he liked Morris Gerrard. He said, "The poor bugger," and he shook his head. I think he feels sorry for Morris but I don't think he likes him. He says Morris has a mean streak.

Rita Gerrard doesn't come to the store very often either but when she does, she wears a big light blue coat that covers up all of her. She wears red lipstick and black shoes with wide heels like my grandma used to wear. She walks hard on the wood floors and you can hear her everywhere she goes. Her face is square and white like bread and it all moves when she talks. My mom's face is small and she is quiet. Her eyes are brown and slanted. Sometimes I think she's sad but then my dad says something to her and her mouth opens wide and her laugh is a surprise. She has straight white teeth and when they show, her forehead shines and her eyes come in close to us. They are shiny then, like her forehead.

We have a big old house, painted white with dark

green around the window frames. The store is right next to us. You can touch the yellow brick wall from our verandah. Sometimes I play tennis against the store wall for a long time. I try to bounce the ball once on our verandah, then hit it against the store when it bounces up and let it bounce once before I hit it back. On this side of the store where the tennis ball bounces, but inside, there's an old wooden rack as high as the ceiling with fifty bins filled with nails and staples and brads and bolts. On the floor there's blue and pink salt blocks for the cattle to lick in the fields. The scale to weigh the nails is old and there's round flat weights to set on to make a balance, but I don't understand it. The scale at the front is easy. I can slice a pound of bacon and weigh it and wrap it in brown paper and snap the string with my fingers now instead of using a knife.

In front of our house we have some rose bushes and some snapdragons and lots of white flowers that are tiny and low to the ground. One of the jobs I have to do is pick up candy wrappers from the yard so it looks tidy. In the summer, on Sundays after supper, the sun goes around to the back yard. I sit with my dad in the front yard and help him pull crabgrass. He runs his hand back and forth through the lawn looking for four-leaf clovers. I like it when he finds them, and most of the time he does. When he doesn't I feel scared that he might not be lucky any more. When someone comes for gas or a quart of milk, I keep looking.

In front of the store, there's two gas pumps. On either side of our house and store there's two houses, two on each side, and two big chestnut trees and mountain ash and maple trees. And then the village ends and the speed signs on either side go up to sixty miles an hour again.

I like to look at people's houses and their lanes and the trees they have and their gardens and their dogs and barn cats and 4-H calves. Other kids have hay mows to play in but they want to come and be in the store. Everybody's house is different. Sarah's house is next to the creek, and they have a pigpen right behind their house that's empty now but we play rodeo there. Her house is like a big old shed and it's got dozens of places to hide in and there's eight kids and Sarah's the oldest and I think she's so lucky but she thinks I'm lucky. I love it when I get to sleep over at Sarah's house. I go in the middle, between Sarah and her little brother Willy, and sometimes Christopher cries to come in with us and then we sleep crosswise in the bed.

I'd be scared to sleep at the Gerrards' house. They don't have grass in front of their house. The corn field goes right up to the back of their house where there's a boarded-up door and no steps down from it. I wouldn't like to live in a house where there was a door you couldn't open, or go in and out from, ever. There's a trap door that goes down to our basement and I don't like it but you can hook the door up to the back kitchen wall so it stays up while you're down there getting a jar of pickles or the Crokinole board.

Tom Gerrard is the oldest. His hair is the blackest black. He combs it straight back off his forehead which is shiny like my mom's when she smiles. His eyes are the bluest blue. He wears jeans and a flannel shirt like all the big boys do. He is sixteen or seventeen like all the grade eight boys. He is tall and we are a little bit scared of him because he smiles at us.

All the big boys that go to our school get up at six to milk cows and shovel out stalls. They pull down hay and corn with black in it from the silos. They have big muscles and pimples. Their hands look dirty and they all poke their compass points into their calluses and when the teacher isn't looking they show us how deep they can push the points into their skin. When they do this they grin at us and at each other. It doesn't hurt them or us. It isn't mean. It might even be good, because it wakes them up. Most of the time they just look sleepy.

They sit at the back of the schoolroom around the big wood stove and they are the ones who bring the wood up from where it's piled in the basement. Big loads of it come in September and they have to carry it from the wagon and stack it all up. There's an axe in the cellar and a chopping block and one of the big boys splits kindling in the morning for the teacher. The boys don't mind. They like chores better than being at their desks. When they're at their desks they stretch their legs out into the aisle and they take their boots off. The heat makes their socks stink and we tell them that but they don't care.

Tom Gerrard doesn't sit near the stove. He put his desk by the windows at the back of the room. He is better than any of the other boys because he can draw horses. First he uses his pencil and then he uses his pencil crayons. Some of the horses are black and shiny. He gets the black to go dark because he turns it on his tongue. He draws pintos and Shetlands. Sometimes he draws just their heads and sometimes he draws them running. He draws Percherons like the team Clancey Davis takes to the fair. Sometimes he draws just their big hairy feet but once after Clancey took our whole school back to his bush by the lake to see how to make maple syrup from sap, Tom drew a whole mural of it on the blackboard. He drew the bush and the little buckets hanging from the trees and the horses and us all standing in the snow around the fire. He drew the outline with white chalk and we all got to colour it in with the box of coloured chalk the teacher keeps locked in the cupboard. I don't see why she has to lock the colours up.

I used to think that Tom liked it when me and Sarah and Lillian watched him drawing but one day he finished a horse picture and he pushed it to the side of his desk. I think he meant one of us could have the picture if we wanted it. But nobody wanted to go first. Tom put his finger on one corner of the page like he was afraid to touch it too. He dragged the paper back across his desk with his one finger and then when he got it to his stomach he scrunched it up with both hands and threw it into the wastepaper basket and then he laughed and his teeth all showed like a horse. I am a little bit afraid of him.

Raymond Gerrard used to come to school but he got expelled. He brought a shotgun to school and before we got there he took the gun and smashed down the Chinese village we were making out of toothpicks and glue and moss and twigs. The police car came to the school and Raymond was sitting in the back seat while the policeman and Mrs. Southerland stood outside and talked. She sent us all inside. My dad said it was time Raymond got away from the farm, that maybe he could work the boats or the mines and it would be better for him and everybody else too.

Doraleen is in the same grade as me and Sarah and Lillian but she is a year older than us. At the Christmas concert I had to be her partner for a song about two girls who have a fight. We had to pull each other's pigtails and stick our tongues out until the last verse when we had to kiss and sing arm in arm. It was the best time I ever had with Doraleen but I was glad when it was over because most of the time she swears if you even look at her. She makes her nose holes flare out and she pretends she's a bull.

Who I like is Freddie, the Gerrards' little brother. He's short and round like a teddy bear and even Doraleen loves him. I always pick him when the teacher tells me and Sarah and Lillian to listen to the grade ones read. Now that it's spring we go outside with the readers and Freddie likes to sit under the row of pine trees. He reads way different than I do. He only knows the words if they're on the same page as he learned them. What we like to do is pick the fresh lime-green buds from the pine trees and shred the buds and make a pile and we call it our crop.

Next week our whole school is going on a bus trip to Niagara Falls and everybody's excited, except for Doraleen. She's not allowed to go any more. Yvette is going to teach us how to yodel. She's going to bring her guitar and she says she'll play it all the way home if we stay awake and sing with her.

After our trip there's just two weeks left of school and I don't think Maura and Ben will come back for the trip or for the rest of the year. If they don't come by Monday, I don't think they'll be back. I hope Maura's mother is nice because I'm not sure if her dad is. He might be mean like Morris Gerrard. We don't really know who they are yet, or where they came from. All we know is that their dad came here to be a hired man for Clancey Davis and he moved them into his old summerhouse back at the lake. I heard my mom say there's no electricity at that house and my dad shook his head as if he was mad at something. He doesn't like Clancey but I don't know why.

Maura and Ben, they only came to school for about two weeks. We don't see them anywhere. Maybe they are fixing their house back at the lake. My aunt has a cottage at the lake and sometimes I bike down there if I'm not too scared to go alone. Sarah and Lillian aren't allowed to go to the lake alone. I just go without asking. Once I saw a whole family of brown rabbits on the grass at my aunt's. I got off my bike and sat down and the rabbits hopped around for a long time. I didn't bother them at all. Maybe Maura will see them. She won't scare them.

Maura and Ben were kind of like the Gerrards, but not really. Ben sort of looked like Raymond used to look before he brought the shotgun to school. His hair was shaved like from the army but he didn't talk in orders or anything. He hardly talked at all, but he was nice to Maura. He watched out for her in between doing his own work. He wasn't sleepy. His handwriting was like Mrs. Southerland's, which is big and slanted and easy to read like the examples on the cards above the blackboard. He hit the baseball really far out into the bean field but he didn't run around the bases. He didn't even bother. I don't know if that's mean or not.

Maura was the most raggedy girl we'd ever seen. She had huge pouty lips and you could see the inside skin of her mouth and she sucked her thumb all the time. Her teeth stuck out. The whole time she was at school she wore the same thing. A red sweater over top of the kind of blouse you wear to church, with a black string bow at the neck. She had a weird skirt with flowers on it and it was short but way too big and twisted around her funny just like her brown leggings were twisted at her ankles. That sounds mean but it can't be mean just to *see*.

I could give her some of my clothes but they'd be

way too big and I don't know if she'd want my old clothes. Maybe it would make her feel worse. I would never give anyone my black dress with the pink and white safety pins printed on. Everyone pinched me when I wore that dress. They said my pins were coming open because I was too fat. Annie Mae, who lives down the road, made it but I picked the material. Now I hate it. Annie Mae lives alone on the hill and she is tall and old and skinny and tilted forward. When she walks with the wind at her back you think she might fall over on her face. She is cranky and says hold still and she doesn't ever smile. She sews for me when we can't find clothes in the catalogue that have an x beside the size. I'm not fat. I am just chubby, my mom says.

Doraleen is big for her age, like me. She wears a brassiere, but I don't need one. Doraleen wears surprises some days, like a string of pearls and red lipstick. It's like she's playing dressup and she is different those days, and she acts like she is better than us. We don't look at her though, because it's embarrassing.

Maura and Ben came to school early on the first day and they had desks and they were sitting in them when we all came in. The teacher told us their names and Ben said hello in a low voice but Maura's head went down on her desk. The teacher left her alone for a while as if she wasn't there, but later in the morning she went over and lifted Maura's shoulders up, and kind of pried Maura's chin up with her thumb. She took Maura's thumb out of her mouth and opened her book and handed her the pencil.

For all the days Maura was at school, she mostly sucked her thumb and turned the pages of her reader from front to back and then started over. Once a day the teacher would take Maura up to her big desk and teach her something. At recess and at lunch, Maura stood by herself at the back corner of the school. She watched her brother play baseball. Once or twice in the first week, Ben would go to her and push her toward us but she put her head down into her sweater like a turtle. We didn't ever laugh at her.

But I think we should of asked her to play. We should of said come and find pine cones. We could of shown her how to play the stone game with us.

Our school is made of stones from all the fields and we are trying to give each stone a name. It is going to take a long time because we walk around and around the school until we find a name that sounds right. The ones we have now are Pot Roast, Sandpaper, Diamond Eye, Starflake, Vomit Stone, Holstein and Angel.

Doraleen says we're stupid. She goes around the school in the opposite direction and she tries to bash us into the walls. She bashed into Maura every time. We went around Maura but we should of taken her hand. I should of but I didn't want to because her hands were wet and wrinkled. She had tiny hands and she had soft bendy nails like Sarah's baby sister's nails. Mrs. Southerland has fingernails that look like toenails and so do the big boys. I still bite my nails but I'm going to quit. My mom says that's how you get worms. Once the Gerrards had ringworm. We heard the Health Nurse whisper it to the teacher and then she took all of them into the cloakroom and told them something. We don't know what. At recess Doraleen chased us around the schoolyard. She tried to rub her arms on us. Her brother Tom grabbed her hair and slapped her face for doing that and then Doraleen went and hid in the stone shed near the fence for the rest of the recess.

The stone shed is really scary. It used to be the bathroom when some of the older kids started school but now we have toilets in the cloakrooms. The boys' smells worse than ours and Doraleen says it's because they piss and miss. There's a picture of Queen Elizabeth in our cloakroom and a picture of King George in the boys'. The teacher keeps the strap in a drawer in her desk but she gives it in the boys' cloakroom. That's where Doraleen got the strap too.

The shed by the fence is scary. It's cement and it's square but it's like a silo. It echoes in there. Sarah's little brother climbed up their silo once when we were supposed to be watching him and he started screaming because he didn't know how to get back down. Sarah climbed up for him so fast. I hate silos and I hate the stone shed at the school. There's a cement wall that divides it into two sides and there's two holes on each side to sit on. It's dark even if you keep the door open. I hate that place.

We don't know what happened to Maura in there. We didn't know she was in there because we were playing the stone game. We were going around and around and we didn't really notice that Doraleen wasn't bumping into us or that Maura wasn't sucking her thumb at the back corner of the school any more. But Ben must of noticed because he was playing baseball and all of a sudden he started running to the shed with the bat in his hand, hollering for Maura. He was running backwards swinging the bat for everybody to stay back. And we did.

We saw Ben shove Doraleen hard against the door and she fell sideways and then got up and ran. Maybe she ran home but I don't think so. I think she hid somewhere safe. We don't know what happened but maybe Maura had to go to the bathroom. We're not allowed to go inside

the school till the bell rings at quarter to one. Maybe
Doraleen scared her. We don't know. Maura was crying
and choking and her face was all dirty. Ben was rubbing
her face on his stomach and swinging the bat back and
forth. Then he threw the bat way off to one side of the
schoolyard and he picked Maura up and lifted her over
the fence and they walked away with all of us watching.

We were going to run and tell the teacher but then
we saw her at the window and she turned away. I hate
Doraleen. She got the strap the next day and she didn't
even cry. She says she wouldn't go to Niagara Falls with
any of us for a million bucks. Doraleen is so loud and so
awful and Maura didn't make any noise at all.

I don't think Maura and Ben are coming back to
school. Their mom and dad came to the store on the
weekend and their dad talked to my dad in the post office.
Then their mom put groceries on the counter. We don't
have carts. She was slow and she got things one box and
bag and can at a time which was good because I am just
learning how to write out bills. She smiled at me once or
twice and I think she's sad but she's nice, maybe. She
doesn't have teeth. They put their boxes in the back of
their old truck and I guess they went to their place at the
lake. It's nice back there and it's nearly summer. My dad
says they'll move on after the crops are off. I hope Maura
can sit in the grass with the rabbits before they have to go.

I think it's mean what happens to almost everybody
whether they deserve it or not. My brother Bob came last
night to help my dad take a truckload of tires into the
basement of the store and they argued about Dad buying
more tires when he's not supposed to work so hard any
more. Bob went into the back yard to have a smoke and I
followed him. We stood behind the woodshed where no

one could see us. I told him what happened last week and how mean it was and he told me something I sort of wish I didn't know. He told me two things. One about Raymond, that Dad gave Raymond a job helping him in the store. I don't remember that but Bob said it just lasted one day because that night before Raymond went home, Dad caught him stealing cigarettes. Then there's the other thing. Bob said it was the meanest thing that ever happened to him when he was my age and it was with his dog, a big brown and white collie named Lad. Bob was outside around the gas pumps cleaning up and Lad was hanging around with him too like he always did. Then Morris Gerrard came to get gas and he got out of his truck and walked around to Bob and kind of ordered him to put in two dollars' worth. Lad growled and then he snapped at Morris's leg but he didn't bite him. Morris had big boots on and he kicked Lad so hard Lad went flying and landed against the brick wall of the store. His back was broken and Dad had to shoot him.

I asked my brother if he still hated Morris Gerrard and he took a long time to answer but he finally said yes, he did. I want to hate Doraleen but what he told me makes it harder. I'm glad her dad isn't my dad and I'm glad it's nearly summer.

The Man With No Voice

Jeremy came home from his paper route today looking a little strange under the eyes, like he might have been crying. Now I think no, he wasn't crying. I think he came home to find out if he could be proud and scared at the same time. He sat down at the kitchen table, 4:30 p.m., the red carrier bag still slung over his shoulder. The skin under his eyes was a bit puffy, that's all.

Joe was in the bathroom, right off the kitchen, fixing the chronic drip in both bathtub taps. He had already fixed the front porch window, which has been broken and patched with plastic since the start of hockey season when Jer's stick went through it in the 5:00 a.m. rush for practice. It's spring. The weather is fantastic, the best spring in years.

How did it start? What did Jeremy say first, while I sat at the table with my tea and my crossword puzzle?

I think he said, "Will somebody please give me a ride to the far house?" He was talking about the one house on his route which is a block away from all the others.

"Hold on a minute and I'll take you," Joe said from the bathroom.

Jer relaxed. Normally he gets an argument from either or both of us: Something wrong with your legs?

"You know that man who can't talk?" Jer asked, running his fingers across his lips, wondering, I guess, what it would be like to have a mouth that didn't do what you wanted it to.

No, I didn't know him. Why?

"He makes sounds like grunts but you can't understand anything."

"I know who he is," Joe said, poking his head around the corner for a second, then disappearing again. Tap tap tap with the pipe wrench on the vice grips.

"He asked me to make a phone call for him," Jer said. "He came out on the porch when I delivered his paper and he asked me to come inside."

"Asked you?"

"He waved his hand," Jer said, showing me the beckoning motion.

"And you went inside his house?"

"He had a blackboard and it said, 'Hi, I'm Uncle John. Please help me.'"

"Oh my God! Jeremy!"

"I felt sorry for him," Jeremy said. "He can't talk. He wanted me to make a phone call for him. There was chalk and he wrote down a number."

Joe stopped fixing and he stood in the doorway, the pipe wrench dangling in his hand.

We've brought our kids up to recognize, anticipate even, when someone needs help, prompted them over and over to show respect, speak when spoken to. Eye contact not head-down. If someone shows interest, be friendly. Etc. etc. We do not dwell on the horrific things that have happened to children who are not wary of strangers. I could never bring myself to say Do not help a man with a broken arm load groceries into his car. Or van. Especially not a panel van. I could never bring myself to say These people know the children who are most vulnerable, most apt to be obedient or kind. The most either Joe or I could or would say was Be careful. Trust your nose.

It's not that they aren't aware of what can happen. It's just that they get so much of it. Abductions in the paper, on the news, pictures of missing children on the milk cartons, posters above the video games in the lobby of Safeway. They must fantasize what moves they'd make. Box kicks, chops, lix.

Both kids went through the Care Kit. Julie first. She made us all laugh with her imitation of the puppet that looked like Kermit the Frog. She would waltz around the room flapping her arms, singing, "Trust your feelings, your body belongs to you," in a high shaky voice.

I don't know where the mute man lives but I know every house on the paper route because I delivered for Jeremy while he was at horse camp for a week. His whole grade five class went after parents took bottle duty for a year, raised $9,000 collecting, sorting and returning pop and beer cans. While Jer was in the mountains upcountry, riding a horse named Paint, learning how to survive in the woods, I walked his route.

I was afraid of dogs. Not shaggy ones like ours, but sleek black ones with yellow eyes. Hounds from hell. Their tails don't wag. Instead, they function as antennas. Before Jeremy got the route, a woman had it, and one day last summer, when I was sitting in the front yard, I heard the paperwoman scream. She had been walking down the pathway to the house two doors from us and the dog there had circled her with its rope, trapped her, and stood baring its teeth, tail straight out. I grabbed the plastic lawn chair I'd been sitting on and ran. A broom would have been better, or maybe a shovel. Better yet, Joe. Anyway, I made some poking and swinging motions with the chair which kept the dog's teeth from us while we untangled the rope. The woman threw her arms around me, sobbing and shuddering, and I put my arm around her waist and walked along the street with her as far as our house. She stayed an hour and told her life story.

She offered to take Jeremy with her on the route for a few days before handing it over. He didn't want to go after the first day. It was easy, he said, and she talked too much. But I insisted that he go *one* more day. "Don't be rude," I said. "You'll hurt her feelings."

The route: a mixture of houses that are meticulously tended amongst those in disrepair, arranged in a continuous bell curve—shabby, building up house by house to the best, and then down slightly and back up again. Ours? Not at the bottom or the top of the curve. Also usually some form of garden with every yard. Rock gardens, back yards with ceramic elves and deer. Do these attract or repel the real deer? Some people drape their flower beds with gillnets but I have resisted, depended on luck, on catching them in the act of devouring my hostas. There are houses sinking into the muskeg, houses with six inches of moss on their roofs. A house with a broken front window, heavy plastic on it all winter long. Don't these people care? Don't they know how much money it's costing them on the gas bill?

"I know that guy," Joe said. "I know where he lives.

I seined with him, years ago. He's all right but you can't trust him. He doesn't pull his weight and he shouldn't have done that, Jer. You shouldn't have gone into his house."

I'd been picturing a house with a fat grey cat on the porch, the one that had three cat dishes to step around. I could see my grey-eyed son on the weathered boards of that porch and I'd invented a sparse-haired, skinny man in an undershirt, his age-spotted muscular arm holding up a small rectangular slate. Help Uncle John. I'd been inching along with this perception of the mute man I'd never seen. He had sandy-coloured hair, sandy-blond, and blondish red hair on his chest and arms. Who knows why I invented this man? It was no one I recognized from the neighbourhood or downtown streets. Where did this man I was tracking come from?

Jer, with his heart in the right place but also in his throat, hesitates but steps over the threshold of the old door. Uncle John shuts it gently, so gently, so as not to scare the boy. It's four o'clock and "Melrose Place" is on his TV and the room is not dark but dim. The old couch is covered with a gold-coloured acrylic blanket. The carpet is indoor-outdoor and the traction is good. He can run. Jer can run. There's time if he uses his head, his nose. I close my eyes and see the phone, the old black phone, desk style, on a veneer-topped end table. The man who can't speak is sitting on the edge of the chair by the phone. His arms are so strong. He is so powerful. He is a boa constrictor readying to wrap himself around my boy.

"He wrote on the blackboard. He wrote 'Call this number and say it's John. Say John wants to see you.'"

"Oh," I said. "Oh. Okay." I released the breath I'd been holding like Houdini under water. What instinct there? To fill the chest, the breast with air, puff up, become large, so the encircling arms would be round a false self, that could then slip through, slip out of the grip. "Were you scared, Jer?" He nodded. "Really scared or just sort of scared?"

"I don't know," he said.

Tap tap tap from the bathroom. Joe, thinking on the pipes. Let Fran do the mother thing.

The tapping stopped. "Jer," Joe said, "I know that guy and he doesn't have many friends. He probably had an emergency and you can't blame him for calling you in off the street when he saw his chance, but it still wasn't quite right. I'm gonna go see him. Just let him know you're not available for phone calls."

"I kept getting the wrong number," Jer said. "I called the number and said the words on the blackboard, 'It's John,' but the guy I phoned, his name was John too, he kept saying 'Hang up, you little bastard.' The man kept writing, 'Try again.'"

"And you did?"

"I felt sorry for him."

"You didn't think that you shouldn't go into a stranger's house?"

"I forgot."

"And then, after you phoned all those times, then what?"

"He opened the door. He said 'Thank you.'" Jeremy imitated how the words sounded coming out and again he touched his fingers to his lips as if this would help him understand what he felt about himself, about the man. There was no tapping in the bathroom.

I found my own fingers at my mouth and then at my forehead working away at the creases there. Back to my silent mouth, a numb voiceless Thank you, thank you in my throat.

"C'mon, Jer," Joe said. "I'll drive you down to the end house."

Joe and I talked about it after Jeremy got his blades on and sped off to play street hockey. "What's your take on it now?" I asked. "After the initial shot in the heart?"

"I think it's okay," Joe said. "Not great, but legitimate. Fair enough. The guy can't talk."

"Mmm hmm," I said. "I think so too. I just don't like this Uncle John business. I wonder if we should just feel out the situation. Ask a cop, maybe. Just feel it out for the sake of other kids."

"Can you do that?" Joe wondered. "Will they give you that information?"

"I don't know," I said.

We decided to wait till Jer has his next baseball practice. His coach, Vern, is a cop. We'll catch Vern after the game, tell him about it without mentioning names, see what he has to say, then go from there.

Fool Such As I

Mern, he says, it's not the end of the world. A year goes by before you know it.

No driver's licence for a year!

He says, you play, you pay, Mern. We were a little impaired that night you got charged, but that's life.

Just play 'er cool for a while, Mern, and before you know it, you'll be back on the road. Lay low for a while. Just ride 'er out.

Not him that can't drive. Not him can't drive anything but a tractor in the corn field for a year. I'd like to see him plow up the fields if he lost his licence. I'd like to see his furrows. I'd like to see him without a jingle in his pockets. He'd be moaning about a man's right to his own roads, a thirsty farmer's right to relax. Have a few beer in his own truck on the roads his taxes pay for. He'd be going on and on and on, cryin' in his beer. Complaining to anybody who'd listen.

Have a good cry, he says. That's what you need. Get 'er all out and be done with it. If I start crying, it'll be pretty goddamn wet!

I'm gonna get back on the road. I just gotta pull up my socks.

My old grandma. If she was alive, I'd go see her. Give her a blast. Wake her up. She'd stick her head out the bedroom window, little fieldstone house on the 10th concession. When I was little, before I went to school, I used to pull a wagon down the road to her house, through all the puddles. Then I'd yank the wagon back and forth on her sidewalk, making muddy tracks, back and forth, back and forth till she heard me.

And she'd yell, you little devil! You sure got devilment in you. G'wan home with that muddy wagon. Don't come back here with that muddy wagon. And I'd pretend to be sorry. Then she'd get a kind of smile on her old mug. You little devil, she'd say. Park your wagon and c'mon in.

I miss her.

It's not much. A year. Not as if I have to stay off the road entirely. I can still get around on the back roads. There's never any cops out here—except that night. We shouldn'ta been on the highway. That's all. Stupid.

Where you folks headed, that cop said. Nowhere in particular, I said. Just driving around seeing whose lights're on and whose're off. Nowhere in particular. There a law? I said.

Law against driving with open beer... 'Fraid I'm gonna have to ask you folks to park your wagon. And there's a breathalyzer here, if you'll just step out of your vehicle, ma'am.

Park my wagon. There's no way. I'm not gonna ask Dunc. Drive me here, drive me there. Pick me up this. Pick me up that. No way. No way I'm calling up the neighbours. You going in to town today? Mind if I tag along? No way. I don't like asking favours. I don't like asking for anything.

My son Jack, next farm over, he says, Mom, you need anything, just ask. Just ask Lorna. His wife. I wouldn't ask Abnormal Lorna for nothing. I wouldn't ask her if my life depended on it. I take enough. Boy can she fight. Argue black is blue. I wouldn't care if I never saw her again. 'Cept for Andrew.

Gram-Maw, he says, Gram-Maw. I'm comin' to see you, Gram-Maw. He cuts through the field in his rubber boots. Two and a half years old. He gets here on his own. Which is fine. Just dandy. The less I see of her, the better.

Dunc says, Mern, I don't know what you got against her. She's just like you. That boy of ours married a woman not unlike yourself.

No way. There's something strange about her. Abnormal. She tries to be funny but she's not. She's not me. And thank God I'm not her. Give her a drink and she's weird. After anything with pants on. I don't go weird. I just like to egg them on. See what they do. Farmers're shy. They get red necks. She's hurting Jack, and I don't like it. The last thing I'd do is ask her for anything.

My sister Bernice, she says I'm asking. She makes me sick. I'm healed, my sister says, but what about you, Mern? You're asking, she says. Not just asking, but begging to be healed. Pardon, I says, pardon me? Well, she says, take a look at yourself. Asking, asking for trouble, asking to be caught. Your whole life, asking for it. You'd better take a look at your life, she says.

And so I stuck my chin out and asked her: Why's that, Bernice? What should I look at, Bernice, that you can see so clear with your new eyes. What?

I heard about you and Dunc, she says. I heard you were cruising around drunk. Now you got no licence. Driving around drunk, asking for it. Again. You're walking through your life with your eyes closed, Mern, she says. And then she closes her eyes and she says, it hurts me to see you.

We had a good time, I says. We didn't hurt nobody. We had a good time. Something she doesn't know how to do. My sister, Bernice. She's a nurse. Lives on a farm outside Wayneston. Sour old Bernice. When I go to see her, I put three spoons of sugar in my coffee. Every time I see her, she's on about the family. She says, Look. Look at us. Adult children of alcoholics. We're all suffering, she says. All out of touch with our inner child that never got loved or something.

You go find your child, I say, but leave me out of it. Leave me out. Mern, she says, I hit a hard place when Pete lost his leg.

I felt like saying he was pretty useless when he had two legs, but I didn't. I guess I could've said it and then told her that was the child in me, crying to get back at her. She's the mean one. She's the one has to spit out all her mean thoughts. Jealous. She's always been jealous 'cos I have a good time. Because everybody around here likes being around me. I got life. Nerve. I get people going. People like me 'cos I loosen them up. They look at me and they let their own wild streak loose. They wag their tails a little. Most people.

What're you asking for, Mern, my sister says. Take a look, she says. I had to. And I feel better. It's hard. What're you fighting?

I coulda said, you, Bernice. You.

You gotta dig, she says. It's hard work but it's worth it.

Pour me a cup of your poisonous brew, Bernice, I said. Fill up my cup and pass the sugar.

You think you're so smart, she says.

I am, I says, I am. I learned how to read and write from Gramma before I started school. I was ahead of you when I started. 'Member? Reach down and dig for that, Bernice.

That's what I mean, she says. I mean you coulda made something besides a fool of yourself. You still could.

What'll I make, Bernice? Beds? Make beds like you? I didn't say that to her. She's so proud she's got a white hat. Good for her with her little white hat! But I don't see her life's any better than mine. I don't see her life or anybody's better than mine.

Call me, she says. Call me if you need some help. Don't be afraid to ask. You hurt, she says, you hurt all over. I know. And then she puts her arms around me. Well. She was asking me to cry. Cry if you need to, she says. I'm here. Well, I said, I'm not in the mood.

I coulda said, You want me to cry, Bernice? You want me to cry, then pinch me. Pinch me like you used to when were kids. Pinch me so hard and then hiss at me and say cry baby, cry baby, cry baby Mern.

Dig, she says. Well I dug up a couple beer and I dug up my old bike, brought it down from the rafters in the drive shed. And I just might get back on the road with it.

If I want to dig I go up in the attic. I got movies up there. I got blue movies, Bernice. Blue ones, pink ones. But it'll be a frosty day in hell before you ever see them. I don't need to see them. They run through me. I don't need to dig.

How about grade nine. First year high school, going in to town on the bus, seventeen miles. Standing at the corner of the 8th concession with Bernice. Waiting for the bus to come along. Plaid skirt, bobby socks, new saddle shoes, tight sweater, neckerchief, new three-ring binder fulla loose-leaf. I guess I got hopes. Bernice, she says, Don't. Don't get your hopes up, Mern. Don't think you look like you're something special, something those town boys are gonna like. 'Cos they won't. They think we're hicks, hayseeds.

I was gonna show Bernice, but she was right for once. Though I never let on, 'cept to Gramma. I mighta discussed it once with Gramma. It was no use talking about it at home. It was pretty bare, that house. Ten of us. And Dad. Dad was a mean old bugger.

Gramma, I said, I hate all those snots in town. They think they're so good. I'm way better lookin' than half of those town girls, but nobody'll dance with me. They don't want me singin' in their stupid glee club. They think their shit doesn't stink. I'm gonna quit.

Mern, Gramma says, you don't like school, then quit. I don't blame you. But you're smart and you got a lotta fight. Don't ever lose it.

Grade eleven, September. What'll I do? How'll I stand it? How'll I get through another year? Bernice and me were standing there bare-legged in our tight skirts waiting for the bus and along comes Dunc on a Harley. We heard he was home from the west to look after his old dad, take over the farm. He roared past us and wheeled around for another look. Gimme a ride, I said. Bernice said, Don't.

Well, we left her in the dust. Rode all over the country that day, and I never went back to school. I went home to pack. And nobody said nothing, didn't even ask where I was going. You think I cared? Think I'm gonna cry about that? No way. And my inner child didn't cry either. Hasn't yet.

We go everywhere, every party, every dance. Mern and Duncan on the Harley. In the '57 Chevy, in the old pickup, riding the tractor, plowing the fields, cutting the mustard. We cut the yellow mustard and the blue flax. Fed the pigs. Butchered them. And we had cows, milking, for a while too. And then his old dad to care for. He wasn't a bad old bugger, just a nuisance. And then I got pregnant.

I lost that first one but that didn't bother me. It wouldn't've if I didn't go and lose the next one too. I was pretty blue for a while. I guess I cried a bit back then over those two babies and then, well I quit crying and started getting bad nerves. Bad nerves instead of good nerve.

Dunc, he cleared a road back through our corn field to the lake. He got a backhoe in and made a road down the banks to the beach. And things were pretty good again. What more could you ask for? A private beach in the summer, lotta sand and sun. I asked for a baby and I got one. We got Iain and then right after, we got Jack.

There's people'd give their eye teeth for what you and me got, Dunc says. There's people in T'rono who'd give their eye teeth for some of our lakefront, he says, but they'll never get a foot of it. Never. This farm'll be in the family forever to kingdom come. There'll never be a German or an A-rab buying Duncan MacAdam's land.

Half the farm's signed over to Jack now. We still have to figure out how to make it fair with the girls. Dunc wants to build them each a cottage. We'll see what they want. Right now they want T'rono. Iain, Jack, Laurie and Deanna.

Iain. On his sixteenth birthday, we gave him the Harley. We even put a friggin' bow on it. I took pictures with the movie camera, Iain riding off in a cloud of dust, the girls prancing around. He got killed a week later. Eight days later, tipped over in the ditch a few miles from the farm. I guess he was taking a turn too fast on the loose gravel. I guess the bike pinned him. I guess. I forget. I wanted him buried back at the lake and Dunc, he said No way, no way, no way.

So outta six kids, we got three. What side do you

look on? I fight. I push myself. What good's I should have, they should have. What good's why me?

If I wanna get blue, get deep down blue, I think about Iain just joining the town pipe band, swinging the drumsticks, marching down Main Street summer Saturday nights. Not crying for my inner child, crying for my dead one.

If I wanna get rosy, rosy and blue, I can take a look at us all back at the lake. Kids running around bare bum. Dunc and me and the picnic spread out on the blanket. Him sitting up, sifting sand through his hands saying, God must love us, Mern. Egg sandwiches and a jug of Freshie for the kids. Jug-a rye and a jug-a water. My jugs. A black strapless suit. Baby oil and iodine tan. Then throwing another log on the fire, the sun sinking in the lake making it pink and orange. And the sun sinking. Larry, Red, Marge, Gordie, Louise, some of our gang singing Do Lord, oh do Lord, do-ya 'member me.

I can look at that any time I want. Happy all summer long, working like hell getting the hay off, hot and itchy and then going back to the lake and year after year feeling good, having fun. And then if I look again, there I am. Sitting on Red's knee. There I am putting sand down his bathing suit. Plastered. There I am snuggled up to Gordie, playing peek-a-boo under a blanket. And there I am with a black eye. There I am with sunglasses.

There's Dunc, face tight as a drum, dukes up, saying slow down Mern, slow down. You're hurtin' me.

Do I wanna look at that? If I got to, I can.

Baby, I said, baby. Try and hurt *me*. Just *try*.

I'd rather look at the girls. There's the Christmas we bought Deanna and Laurie guitars. We had a bunch of people in and the girls sat behind the tree to sing their carols, too shy to sit out front. In the movies you can just see their feet stickin' out. Little bit of white from their blouses.

Laurie left home. She went off to university in T'rono. I missed her but I still had Deanna. Deanna, then she up and says, Mom, I hate school. I'm quitting. I'm gonna get a job and live with Laurie, she says. Not sixteen yet.

Wait, I said. Wait a year. Just a year. No way, she said, I'm going and you can't stop me.

Please, I said. I said please. Didn't make no difference. Please.

Same as you, Dunc says, same as you. Saying please never stopped you.

Laurie, she takes psychology. Archaeology, and a couple more ologies. Works part time in a muffin shop. Deanna, she got a job at the Silver Dollar. Good music there. Country music in the city. Sometimes she gets a chance to sing. She sent us a tape of the song Dunc always asks her to sing, had it done on a karaoke machine. "Heaven's Just a Sin Away," that's the name of it. I'd like to see her standing up on the stage. I guess she's got nerve but it took her a while to get it. I don't know.

I'm gonna go see them. Whether they want it or not, I'm going. I'm not gonna call and say Please come home. I'm gonna call and say Go get a case of Canadian. Get two. I'm coming down. No, I'm not driving. No. I'm not in the mood for driving. I'm gonna take the bus, get on the Greyhound. Express to T'rono.

In the meantime, I'm gonna fix up this bike. Maybe wheel in and see Abnormal. Shock the shit outta her. Better than cryin', eh Bernice. Better to stir up a little shit than start cryin'. If I start cryin', it'll be pretty goddamn wet.

On the Road

Our old station wagon was jammed and so was an ancient trailer which had served as our tool shed for the last five years. Speaker columns, amps, two guitars, a banjo, a mandolin, boxes of harmonicas, cords, batteries, suitcases and duffel bags, a portable gas barbecue, amphibious tubes—the kind that work on both snow and water—you name it, we'd packed it, and we were ready to go.

We had emptied the trailer the night before. Light line, heavy rope, life preservers, life vests, a survival suit, two or three pairs of caulk boots, assorted sizes of gumboots, hip waders, heavy and light tarps, shovels, picks, mallets and buckets, lumber, peat moss, slug bait, garage sale rejects. It was like dismantling layers of our life, a midden. Next we moved the trailer from the lawn to the driveway. This involved fetching 4x12s from the pile of lumber in the deep back yard, and using these as tracks and levers to roll and lift the wheels. It was satisfying to see that such heavy-duty labour could be accomplished with will and ingenuity. We took Woof, his blanket and his squeaky rubber bone to the SPCA, and assured the kids that this holiday would be good for the dog. A break, some new friends. He'd think our home was paradise after he came home.

Before the night was over, Joe had hooked up the trailer to the bumper of the car and packed his equipment in it. The car was ours to fill and we did.

All that remained for the morning was the wiring of the signal flashers from the car to the rear lights on the trailer. Joe recruited a neighbour after an hour or so of frustration. And just as the kids had begun to mope around asking when we'd ever leave, there was a shout. "We got 'er, Fran."

The kids put their beside-them-in-the-car bags filled with things to do and eat in the back seat. They had already argued and flipped on who'd get which side of the car on the ten-hour trip to Prince George. A holiday. A working holiday for Joe, who had a three-week gig at a hotel called the Loggers' Arms, but still, a holiday. Eleven a.m. The fog had burned off. The day was clear and warm.

The garbage was out, the lights were off, the doors were locked. We were ready to get into the car. Almost ready, except for one thing. Joe wanted to drive around the block a couple of times. "Wait here," he said.

When he came back, he was frowning. "Fran," he said, "I want you to jump on the trailer hitch." He bounced on the spot with the heel of his hand.

The kids came running. "We'll do it," they said.

"No," said Joe, "just your mother. I want her to see something."

Holding on to the trailer for balance, I jumped half a dozen times. The whole outfit seemed pretty bouncy to me. "What's supposed to happen?" I asked.

"Look," said Joe. "Look at the bumper. It's not going to hold. It's not strong enough. If we hit a rut on the highway, the trailer could break loose. It could kill someone."

"So could I," I said.

Joe backed into the driveway, unhooked the trailer, unpacked, repacked, and drove off alone. The kids hugged him but I didn't.

Joe called collect at three in the morning. He sounded happy. He'd found the hotel and set up in the bar. Would be starting at six and playing till ten every night except Saturday when the owner wanted an afternoon session too. He'd just come from checking out the other bars in the downtown area. He'd had a hot dog, a Bavarian smoky, at the street vendor's stand. Why didn't they sell good old ordinary hot dogs any more?

"And you," he said. "How's by you?"

No comment.

"C'mon up," he said. "Check the train schedule. Check the bus. Just get here. The rooms in this place sure aren't fancy but we can have three of them. The only other person who's upstairs is one of the barmaids. It's kinda her space but she says she doesn't mind. She's okay. You'll like her. There's a kitchen and a sitting room. We can be comfortable for the amount of time we'll want to spend here. The weather's great. C'mon up. There's no phones in the rooms so I'll call tomorrow around noon. Fran?"

I hung up. I didn't want to stay in a dive. We'd packed the tent, and I'd looked into cabins on a lake outside of the city. "Let's just leave it open," Joe'd said. "Play it by ear. I don't want to drive out to a lake after a gig if I've had a few drinks. It's not worth it. I don't wanna book a cabin or a campsite without seeing it first. It's gotta be safe if you guys are gonna stay there alone some nights."

"Okay, okay," I'd said. "We'll wing it. We'll play by ear."

In the morning I called Via. There was a train at noon that day arriving in Prince George at midnight, the next train two days later. Yes, the kids wanted to go and so did I. Okay, let's hustle. I left a message at the bar for Joe: Arriving midnight.

We got on the train with our bags and books and snacks. I had a deck of cards and I taught the kids how to play blackjack. We used pennies. At one point, a fresh-faced woman who might have been a model for an apple advertisement stopped to watch us. She said she had a brother who'd gambled away his home, his business, his family. We smiled at her as she moved away toward the next car.

"Why did she tell us that?" Jeremy asked as I dealt the next hand.

"She thinks this is a bad game," I said.

"Is it?" Jer asked.

"Bad for some people," I said. "But not for us."

"We're playing for pennies, not houses," Julie said.

"Right," I said. "Exactly."

We couldn't sleep, but the boredom of the trip dropped away as night fell. About half an hour from Prince George we could see the city glowing, its pulp mills creating a foggy yellow halo in the sky. We pressed ourselves into the wide, clean windows as if we could see better what lay ahead but of course we saw only our own faces.

We watched for Joe as the train huffed into the station. We expected to see him shouldering his way through the crowd but he didn't appear.

How could it be so hot at midnight?

"Where's Dad? Why isn't he here?"

"Don't worry. Take your bags and go into the can and change into the coolest thing you can find. Put your bathing suit on under your shorts if you want, Jule. I'll phone the hotel."

Ten rings and finally an answer. "We're closed," a man said. "Locked up two hours ago. I'm the cleaner. I don't know nothing about your husband."

I explained that he expected us, that I was at the train station with two tired kids. I'd take a cab. Would he watch for me and let me in so I could get them settled?

"I can't watch for you," he said. "But you can bang on the door when you get here."

The cab driver raised his eyebrows when I asked for the Loggers' Arms. "The L.A.? Been there before?"

"No," I said. "My husband's playing there. He got here last night."

"He a big fella? Wears a cap?"

"Mmm hmm."

"I took that fella out to the Road Runner on the highway about an hour ago. No way he was expecting company."

"Has it been this hot for long?" I asked.

"Hot as hell," the driver said. "Here we are, Mrs. I'll just wait till you see if you can get in."

The L.A.: a two-storey building with no windows on the ground floor. A small overhead swinging sign, still now in the hot night. A steel door with a face-sized window, wire mesh covering it. The kids' sweaty hands gripped mine. Not the time or the door for a polite rap with the knuckles. Make a fist and pound. Too bad I wasn't wearing those steel-toed caulk boots we'd emptied from the trailer. Laugh a little. Laugh so the kids know it's okay. Laugh at yourself for being so stubborn. It will be funny soon. If not tonight, tomorrow. Or the next day.

We heard bolts slip and clank. The door opened and there stood two of the strangest people I'd ever seen, looking at us as if we were the three strangest they'd ever seen. The woman holding a push broom had eyes like hard-boiled eggs. They were huge and protruding, had red lines running through the whites toward the pale blue yolks. She had yellow-white hair. The man—my attention was torn between his hair, a shiny perfect pompadour, the tattooed intertwining pythons on his forearms, and the set of keys dangling from a chain at his waist. A dog snarled and scratched against an inner door as if he'd destroy himself if he couldn't get at us.

"I don't know," the woman said. "He knows you're coming?"

"Well, we had a fight," I said, trying to lighten up a bit, "but we don't hold grudges."

She looked from Pompadour to us, then back to Pompadour. "I guess it's all right. You take them up, Al."

Up. Up past plaster walls, cracked, bashed in, up beyond the snarling dog, up wooden steps creaking. A bare bulb at the top of the landing, Al's keys rattling as we followed him down the hot, dark and dusty hall. He stopped in front of an open door. The radio played Dwight Yoakam's "Turn It On, Turn It Up."

"This might be it," he said, feeling the inside wall for a light switch.

A double bed, a couple of old dressers, and clothes all

over the place, sweaters, blouses, dresses, makeup, coffee cups—and on the wall next to the bed, two framed pictures. An old one, three kids lined up in front of a house, and a new 8x10 of a young woman with a baby on her lap.

"No, " I said. "This isn't it."

"Fuck," he said. "I don't think this is right."

"Try another room," I said.

This will be funny soon, I thought. It's funny right now except it's so hot. We'll find Joe's room and he'll be sleeping or he'll be back soon.

"Wait here," said Pompadour. He tried two more doors, poked his head in, closed them. Next one, jackpot.

"This is it," I said. "Joe's here."

An unmade bed with a skinny brown cover, his shirts hung on hooks by the door, his books, newspapers, half a submarine sandwich, mustard packets, half a bottle of rum, tins of Coke, an overflowing ashtray. One window, propped open with a stick, overlooked the parking lot. A man yelled, "Fuck you, bitch," and a bottle shattered against the curb. A woman screamed and tried to run. When she fell, he helped her up and they stumbled along together again.

The kids, who'd been quiet till now, began to cry. "Dad said this was a nice hotel," Julie said. "It's so ugly. Why did he tell us to come? How could he lie like that? What if we can't get out? What if he doesn't come back?"

I unbuttoned my shirt and peeled their tops off. "Lie down," I said. "Rest. Sleep. Please sleep." I poured a drink, downed it, poured another one and set the only chair by the window. I turned out the overhead light, turned on the gooseneck lamp on the dresser. Joe'd covered the bulb with tinfoil. "Sleep," I said, blowing smoke out the window. "Sleep. Dad'll be here when he gets here."

"I'm too hot," Julie whined.

"I have to go to the bathroom," Jer said.

"Okay. You guys stay here. I'll see if I can find it."

"Don't leave us here alone," Julie said, alarmed.

We opened the door, peeked out down the hallway. "Prop the door open," I said. "Don't let it shut in case we get locked out." We went a little ways but then I lost my nerve and we turned back.

"You're gonna pee in this Coke can, Jer. We won't look but if you have to go it's gotta be in this can or out the window." My hands were shaking now. Joe, you'd better bloody get here. If he came down the hall with this woman he said I'd like, if I heard them talking, maybe laughing, even if it was in all innocence, if they'd just happened to meet at the front door, come back to the hotel at the same time, what would I do? And then, a key turned in the door, the door opened and Joe's eyes opened wide. He had a pizza box in his hands. "Jeez I'm glad you guys made it," he said. "We're gonna have a great time... What's wrong?"

We took a tour of the upstairs, bathroom first. It was big, clean and smelled of papaya shampoo. Down the hall in the opposite direction, a kitchen with a half-size fridge sitting on the floor, empty but for a head of lettuce, a cucumber, a tomato—salad things—and a quart of skim milk. The sitting room off the tiny kitchen had a TV and a stereo, an exercise bike, a lumpy couch with crocheted blankets and pillows. A coffee table scattered with magazines, tabloids, the city daily. "Where's the tenant?" I asked.

"Amanda? She's on days off. I think she said she was gonna go to Quesnel. Isn't this great? All this space?" The kids began to yawn.

"The dog?" I asked.

"He goes home with the cleaners," Joe said. "I asked about that. They drop him off at the owner's place."

We checked out the kids' rooms. One had a desk. The other had a closet and a dresser that might have been pretty once. Clean sheets and pillowcases? Yes. The owner's wife had made the beds that day in case we came. No, he didn't get my message.

"I think you need your head examined," I said, but really, I felt okay.

The dog was a pit bull. That first morning while we slept with our doors open he'd sniffed around us then retreated to his lair—the office, where his master Bruce did his books. Or so we found out later that morning when the two of them poked their noses into the kitchen while we made toast with Amanda's bread. Use anything you like, she'd told Joe, as long as you replace it.

Bruce and the dog sized us up as we passed the butter and jam. Did he want us here? Would this fellow get through the gig? Could he keep things in line upstairs and down?

"My God," I said. "How long has that dog been here?"

"He won't bother you," Bruce said. "He's trained to bark and attack only at certain doors. Even if you and your kids were robbers, if you're sitting here in the kitchen or sleeping in the rooms, he'll leave you alone. Now if you step one toe into my office when I'm not there, he'll be at your throat.

"What's your kids' names?" Bruce asked.

"Julie," I said. "Julie's ten and Jeremy, he's seven."

"You kids, c'mere. This here's Pepper. He likes kids." Pepper's stub tail waved slightly. "He won't hurt you. C'mon here and pet him."

They were fascinated by that white, short-haired dog with the tan patch over one mean squinty eye. They patted him tentatively at first, one touch at a time on his muscled loins, one pat to his head followed by his snout investigating them. I patted Pepper too. Better a friend than an enemy.

"Can we take him to our rooms?" Julie asked.

"Sure," said Bruce. "Call him and he'll follow you. He likes to run. We run him ten miles a day behind the truck."

"Don't get that dog excited," Joe said in a quiet voice.

"I see you're all set up in the bar," Bruce said. "We'll catch you later."

"Weird hours," I said. "Six to ten."

"No," he said. "Good hours, if you knew anything about my clientele. I take them in early when they're most likely to have some money and get them out before the trouble starts. Pepper, he's my bouncer." He laughed, called the dog, and the two of them went to their office.

The first thing the kids wanted to do was go to the mall. It is a big one, three times the size of the mall in our town. There's a gigantic K-Mart at one end and a medium-sized Sears outlet on the other. In between, it is like the main floor of any mall, minus the bubbling fountains, but with all the same chain stores. When you first go in, your heart beats a little faster, adrenaline surges. What is it possible to bring home, to own?

Julie and Jeremy had $50 each. "Don't blow it all in one shot," Joe said. "Look around, see what there is."

I'd applied and gotten a Sears credit card before the holiday and I felt rich. We've had Visa, but our way of paying wasn't to their liking—i.e. run it to the limit during the off-season, when there's no money from fishing, and pay all $4,000 off the first (well, maybe the second) good week of sockeye. I used to argue with the people on collections, overdue payment duty, used to try to explain that not everyone got regular paycheques for predictable amounts, tried to explain that money came in cycles sometimes, but they never wanted to hear any of that. Put the minimum down each month. Make any kind of payment. I guess I was a little too mouthy once. The next time I used the Visa—handed it to a young gas station attendant—it was "seized."

Julie wanted a new pair of sandals, and beads. Was there a craft store in the mall? She knew what her money would buy. Jer wanted everything—roller blades, balls, gloves, sticks, pads. He'd entered the mall with winged heels, a balloon of hope around him. I found him later slumped on one of the benches where shoppers rest.

I wanted a bathing suit and spent my time in my credit card store where there were racks of them promising concealment of flaws, tummy tuck, full-figure flattery. Like Jer, I was full of hope too. When I'd narrowed it down to three suits, Julie came along and I was glad to see her. "Which is better?" I asked, modelling for her. "They're all nice," she said, "but the blue-green one lights up your face."

Joe bought a cane. A skookum wooden cane. "That dog," he said. "I don't trust him."

We bought groceries, picnic type food, some cereal, plastic cutlery. We made a lunch on the banks of the Nechako River. It was milky green and ran fast. "No, not even wading at this spot," I said. "You'd be swept away."

"Look," said Joe, throwing a branch into the water at the edge. It swirled a half turn and was gone.

And so we were cautious on the banks of that river but we stayed all afternoon, walked until we found a shallow spot and picked stones with Julie who was already thinking of ways to transform her room.

Amanda returned from her days off, and I liked her immediately. She was around my age, early forties, maybe a bit older, a few more times around the block. More weary (a grandma, it turned out), more ready for whatever life threw at her. Going it alone with her own truth. I admired her. She reminded me of, oh, I don't know, a Roseanne raised in northern BC, and of some of the friends I've kept over the years, talked with—the keeper friends who insist on going for the bottom line, keep on coming to terms with who they are and how they feel whether anybody likes it or not. This hotel was a short stop in Amanda's life. She didn't like it but she was almost ready to go. No rent upstairs and pretty good money downstairs. She could handle all the assholes, including Bruce.

She was dieting, sick of being thirty pounds overweight, she said. She was on the wagon. No booze—soda and fresh lime her drink now. She'd bought the exercise bike with a paycheque. Fresh fruit and veggies, four ounces of broiled skinless chicken once a day. She'd switched from Player's filter to a low-tar brand, and smoking them was hard work. I said I'd tried to go cold turkey on all my vices at once lots of times but I never lasted longer than a day, two at most. "Yeah," she said, "but I'm gonna do it this time."

She was good about us invading her space, said go ahead, use whatever you want. Stereo, TV, go ahead. She gave the kids five bucks each. "Go get chips and gravy and a Coke on me," she said.

In the first week, once the kids were settled in bed and before Joe came up from the bar, I used to go to the kitchen and get a beer, take it back to our room. One night Amanda said, "Whyn't you sit down?"

She'd owned the first pet shop in the city and sold the business for a good profit. She'd gotten into the restaurant business, had three kids and a half a dozen foster kids and they all worked with her after school and on weekends. She heard from some of the foster kids, usually when they needed cash, and she usually sent it. "What the hell, eh? It's only money." She had a stash together again, just about, anyway, and she was looking for a good place to open a sandwich bar. Just lunches. Something simple.

She was divorced. He'd worked at one of the pulp mills, still worked there. She was sure he always would. "He likes a regular paycheque, three weeks' holidays and no surprises." She stopped talking, dragged hard on one of those skinny cigarettes and stubbed it out. I pushed my pack of DuMaurier toward her. She shook her head. "I'm hard to please, I guess. As soon as something's going good, I get restless."

She went to the fridge, got out a bag of celery and started scrubbing the stalks in the sink. I opened another beer.

Joe came up the stairs and leaned into the kitchen. "Not working tonight?" he asked Amanda.

"I'm on days now," she said.

"Kids're sleeping?"

"Yeah," I said. "We had a good night after you went to work. We hit the library and the town pool has two big water slides. I did five laps in my new bathing suit. I feel great. Clean. Almost skinny."

"I wonder..." Joe began.

"G'wan," Amanda said, "The kids're fine with me."

The routine was established. From that night on we followed it: we ate our toast or bagels or cereal in the kitchen in the morning. While Joe and I had coffee, the kids played with Pepper. The human Pepper usually popped in to say good morning and chat for a minute. Our one topic was his dog.

He had paid $700 for the dog and it was worth every cent. Better by far than a gun to keep the lid on. He told us about the day his safe wouldn't open. He called a locksmith, gave him directions, then got busy in the bar. When he came back upstairs, he'd forgotten about the locksmith but there he was, frozen on the spot. Pepper had had him cornered for half an hour.

"We have a dog," I said one day. "His name is Woof. He's a Maltese terrier and some other things. We got him at the pound in exchange for a stray cat the kids wanted to keep. He has a beautiful temperament. Spunky. Smart. End of story." I had to stop because I was out of breath from forcing words out against the wall of Bruce. "Why bother?" Joe said after Bruce left.

After breakfast we'd get in the car and find a place to be, away from stores, away from the hotel. A day along the river, a day at a lake where there was a warning sign about "Duck Itch" and how to avoid it by using the fresh water pump every time you got out of the water. A day in Barkerville, the gold rush ghost town/museum.

In Barkerville the kids and Joe panned for gold in troughs set up and run by a professional panner in a black cowboy hat. I took pictures of him teaching Joe and the kids the motions, the patient shuffling of sand. People milled around, some of them obnoxious and demanding in the way that tourists can be, straining and squeezing and elbowing in for every penny's worth of their dollar. The pro weaved through the crowd with an attitude, stopping here and there, to encourage, to crack a joke, or lay his hand under a wrist until the motion was understood. It was as if he had a stake in the experience. "Carter," I whispered to Joe.

Joe nodded, and kept nodding. Carter is the bar manager of a hotel at home, a place some people call the Bucket of Blood. It isn't. No pit bulls, human or otherwise.

We had supper early every night, around five, before Joe went to work. When he left us, we walked to the pool, swam for two hours. Every couple of days, we'd stop at the Inn of the North to use one of the phones, sit on the cushioned purple velvet stools, have our private, plush-carpeted conversations with grandparents there, instead of standing on the concrete-floored lobby of the L.A. using the single phone on the battered wall outside the barroom door, hand cupped to ear for insulation from the noise.

As time went on, I felt I didn't belong in the Inn. The groomed and uniformed front desk staff kept an eye on the kids and me, and I anticipated a night when one of them would approach us quietly and say the phones were for guests only. It began to be a "trip" just to walk on the carpet and we would laugh once we were out the door, at the tingling feeling in our toes.

I never once sat down for a drink in the L.A. Joe did his time and got out. He said everyone who drank there was either fresh out of prison or heading back there soon, unlike our home bar with the rough reputation—some of this, yes—but also some other thing—sometimes—descends, comes down from some heaven—a collective soul—some blessing on us all in a safe place for tears and memory. Home, the pain I was used to, seemed a far kinder place than this, the Loggers' Arms. There were no grandmothers in their best dresses in the L.A. asking their daughters, their granddaughters for a waltz, asking a niece, "Are you yourself now?" and being heard, point taken, the niece switching to coffee or slowing down at least some of the time.

After our nightly swim, we got in the habit of walking the downtown streets in the vicinity of the L.A. On Friday nights the stores were open late and we'd leave the pool early to wander in and out of the shops which were far more interesting than those in the mall. Tee shirts $75 in one place and tee shirts for $2 two doors down. There were many secondhand stores with pots and pans and knives and tents, tree planters' gear heaped up in the windows.

"Why does everyone look so bruised here?" Julie asked one night. We'd just avoided a collision with a woman whose face was swollen, black and blue. She stared at us boldly, dared us to look at her. I wished at that moment that I could ask her to sit down with us on one of the street benches, buy ice cream for all of us.

We looked too long or not long enough, I don't know which, and she spat and swore at us. Before that, outside the liquor store, we'd seen a man crawling. The siren sound came nearer and soon he was lifted off the paved parking lot onto a stretcher.

At the end of our block there was a cafe and gallery-gift shop. Sometimes before going home we stopped there and ate hot apple-rhubarb crisp with whipped cream. They had magazines and newspapers that you could take to your table that sent a no-hurry message. Relax. There was a mix of people we didn't see anywhere else. Once the kids spotted a children's writer who'd been to their school. They got autographs on paper napkins.

As we neared the hotel to go in for the night, we'd hear Joe's deep voice, his guitar.

> He had a blue wing tattooed on his shoulder
> Well it mighta been a bluebird, I don't know
> But he'd get stone drunk and talk about
> Alaska Salmon boats and 45 below.

"Dad has a hard job, doesn't he?" said Jer.
"But he likes it," Jule said.

By the last week, Julie had acquired hundreds of beads, all the paraphernalia that goes with making necklaces and earrings, as well as a collection of river stones, and wildflowers and grasses. She'd picked through remnant bins in the fabric shops and hung the pieces on her walls with push pins, laid a long strip down the centre of her dresser. She had a little cottage industry going, hung her creations on the walls. Amanda took Julie's wares into the bar in a cigar box Julie had lined with turquoise corduroy and set them by the cash register. Each day she sold out, brought the coins to Jule, and Jule bought more beads. Julie wanted to make a special matching set for Amanda before we left and I admired the way she got information from Amanda about colours and designs she liked.

Joe and I went out for a short while on the night Julie finished the gift. We were on our way home when we heard the now familiar sirens and saw that this time, the ambulance was outside the L.A. Joe grabbed my hand and we began to run. When we got to the door, there was Julie sitting at the bottom of the stairs. "Where's Jeremy?" I said as Joe ran up the stairs. "Sleeping," said Jule. "He's sleeping.

"I called 911," she said. She shuddered and her poor dear big blues were almost like the eyes of Egg Lady, the cleaning woman we'd never seen since that night we arrived. "Oh Mom, please. Please. Please don't let her be dead."

"Who?" I said. "Who?"

"Amanda," Jule said and her whole body seemed to go into spasms. I had to clamp my jaws together to hold myself. She reached for my hand and she squeezed it tight, so tight. And then she let go again and she began to make fists of her fingers, closing them and opening them and closing them again.

I put my arms around her, drew her in close. Jule flexed her fingers again. "I finished the necklace and the earrings and I wrapped them and I just wanted to give them to her," Jule said. "I could hear the TV so I thought it would be all right if I went down during a commercial. She had a rubber thing around her arm and she had a needle and she pushed it in and then she saw me. Oh Mom. Her eyes rolled up into the back of her head and her whole body was jerking. I ran down here and phoned 911. I didn't know what else to do. I was afraid to go back upstairs."

A few stragglers had gathered on the sidewalk. "What's goin' down?" a man asked, grinning stupidly. We stared at him and he backed away.

"Oh Mom," Jule said, "we've got to leave here right now. We've got to go home. Dad can't stay here. Oh Mom, is Amanda dead? Did she kill herself because she lived here too long?" We sat until Joe came down, a sleeping Jeremy in his arms. He'd stuck Jer's aquasocks into the back pocket of his blue jeans. He passed Jer over into my arms and lifted Julie into his. "C'mon," he said, "let's walk a bit."

After we'd gone a few blocks, Joe said softly, "Junk."

And a little ways on, "She'll pull through."

The next day I took a bouquet of flowers and a card we'd all signed to the hospital. Amanda was sleeping and I didn't want to wake her. I wanted out of that hospital, that hotel, that city. The sooner the better. As I tiptoed out, Amanda spoke.

"Chip," she said. "I usually just chip. I'm careful... I'm sorry your daughter had to see me."

"So am I," I said.

"Tell her I'm sorry," she said.

"I will," I said, "And you take care."

"Yeah," she said, turning her head away.

"Thanks for sharing your space."

"Some space," she said. "*You* take care. And give Julie a hug." She opened the drawer in the bedside stand and pulled out a twenty. "Give her this. She earned it."

"Does anybody in your family know you're here? Do you want me to call someone?"

"My daughter was here this morning. She's coming back with a milkshake."

We had two more days and we stayed at a little place with cabins and sand and water with no duck itch in it. We decided we could all fit somehow into the car for the trip home, no matter how cramped it was.

Do You Luv Me

On a July Sunday night, Veronica stepped outside the bar where she works and saw what she expected to see, a sky still filled with light even though it was after nine. She'd booked off early because business had dwindled out to just a few old men sipping and a table of women, cannery workers, who really deserved a good long sit and a few more jugs of beer. Soon the plants would be in full production, around the clock, and a day off would be hard to come by. When the last of the fishermen left the bar to head out to the grounds for the 6:00 a.m. gillnet opening, the Sunday summer emptiness had hit. Everyone with something to do had gone to do it. Veronica had poured herself a draft and phoned home. She intended to spring for Chinese or pizza, whatever Roy Jr. wanted. She'd let the phone ring a dozen times and then poured one more draft, but didn't touch it. She'd set it on the waiter's tray and signed out.

What she wanted was a hot bath, to get into a hot hot tub and soak her legs, her feet, her back. Everything ached. She felt the vague indefinable remorse, loss (loss of what?), that always arrived with a hangover.

She stood outside the bar, looking up and down Main Street for a sign. If one of the new white cabs drove by she would flag it. She remembered talking to a driver in the bar last night. He'd said the cab company had done some research and found out that white cars looked cleaner than black ones, showed less dirt. And so he had a new, never-needed-to-be-washed cab. They'd laughed about that. But anyway, none was in sight. She would walk home to the two-bedroom wartime house she shared with Roy Jr. and maybe he would be home. She would fix herself and this fifteen-year-old boy of hers a bowl of chowder, simmer that chunk of halibut Grady had laid on her last night. Had she put it in the fridge? She must have. Those habits don't leave you even if you've had a few too many. She would get Roy to peel the potatoes while she fried the onion and bacon. She would be able to talk to him, say Roy, let's start over. Can you do it? Can you see it? If we could. She would massage this lean handsome boy's tight shoulders, so taut all the time now, till she felt his tension give in to her fingers, till she felt his shell become flesh she knew again, her blood running through him, warm. She would not nag, cry, beg or scream. She would thaw him out, draw him into belief in her, in the two of them. And if, if she spoke softly and patiently and could meet his eyes, stay fixed as they looked through into and beyond her (spooky, spooky as if he knew far more than she about both of them), if she met him calmly, softened him with her own softened and sorry eyes, maybe he would tell her the truth. And the two of them could go from there.

Still, as she walked down Main Street this summer

night, almost able to smell the frying bacon and the fish stock in the pot, she realized she was walking too fast. Roy hadn't been home ten minutes ago and he hadn't been home last night when she'd called around 10:00 or at 2:30 when the bar closed. She was walking too fast on such a beautiful night to get home to an empty house. If she took a roundabout way home through the downtown blocks before heading up the hill, maybe she'd run into Roy. She was so lonesome for him, for what he used to be, full of questions about how everything worked, quick to laugh, gullible, quick to cry. Quick again to recover.

Usually this soft moodiness Veronica felt now, this loving, tender-sorrowful mood descended only when she had finished work, after the bar closed, when the staff united. They were a family, a family all-mixed-up but strong too, drawn together by both the need for the job and the love of it. The drama, the potential drama and danger and love and jealousy and sometimes kindnesses, sometimes really funny, ridiculous things. Seeing and hearing, watching all night long and finally, doors locked, going over the highlights together with these brothers and sisters after closing. This time of night, when they did unite—which wasn't always, wasn't even that often—it was worth enduring all the other nights. And then sometimes it was hard to get one staff drink down for all the sorrow welling up, for all the tragedy that everyone was caught in. It wasn't that there wasn't love—there was. But it was as if there wasn't enough time or money to satisfy yourself and another two or three or even one other person. Sometimes people just got small and desperate and caught in their own need to laugh and forget.

Before she'd booked off tonight she'd watched a couple go through the motions. She'd wanted to go and shake them both, shake some sense into them. They were both beautiful, solid, round and strong, and old too, in their sixties. When they came in they were one. A couple stopping in for a few drinks before heading out to the grounds. They were laughing, the man's arm around her shoulders. They'd had to part to get through the door and they'd laughed and offered each other first entrance. But the woman got slower and sad and the man got stronger. He moved around the bar, talking fish, shaking hands here and there, hugging old friends that he hadn't seen from one season to the next. The woman lifted her head higher and higher but the laugh lines around her mouth turned down and down, dropping like a fu manchu, and she didn't move from her chair except to go to the washroom once. After a time, her husband came back from his rounds, chest out, reaching for her, asking her to dance, but she couldn't rise to him. Tears started running down her cheeks. And then he got her mixed up with a dog maybe he once had and loved, and he tried to bring her out of her sadness, ruffling at her face with his big hands, as if she had a snout and maybe some fur too.

Then there were the women, mostly the young ones—the ones her age too tired too wise too burnt to be bothered—who liked to see what would happen when they danced tight and sexy and too long with another girl's man. Veronica saw people hurting each other, hurting themselves, but she had also been around long enough to know, to believe that these same people forgave, patched it up, carried on. Some died, some killed themselves, some got killed, most carried on.

Veronica and Roy Sr. had carried on for a few years much like the couples she now sees clearly and shakes her head at. What did it matter whose fault it was? And what, once you'd come so far down the road of pain and payback, were the chances of taking some different road together? Veronica and Roy had carried on and then after one final big blowup, Roy said he was moving out. He threw some clothes into a suitcase and tipped over a couple of chairs to make sure she got the point. He was gone, man. And just to make sure he knew she didn't care, she heaved some dishes and a lamp at him, opened the door he'd slammed and threw them smashing on the sidewalk. It had felt good, this rage. And then bad, and then somehow, life was just better without him around. Except maybe for Roy Jr. who, until lately, continued to be himself, open and talkative, except when she brought up the topic of his father. On that subject he had always been a brick wall.

Roy Sr. was a carpenter, which meant he had steady work for half the year and collected UI for the other half. He lived in an apartment on the east side of town, and had stayed single, like she had. He had taken to wearing dress pants instead of jeans, a sports jacket rather than a sweatshirt, and for some reason this embarrassed Veronica as if she had kept him from his true nature.

Roy Sr. had money now. At first she'd assumed it was because he was doing a few jobs under the table, but then she'd heard he was dealing. It didn't surprise Veronica because he'd flirted a bit with coke and so had she, but then of course they'd had no money and that caused more trouble than it was worth. On and on. So. Okay, let him do his thing. Whatever it was. He was giving the boy more money, had lately bought him two pairs of shoes, low suede skater shoes and basketball runners. That must have cost him $250 easy. She'd told Roy she thought it would be better if the boy got a job, earned some of the things he wanted, but Roy said there weren't any jobs, and he'd rather give the kid what he needed than have him ripping people off. He didn't want his son breaking into houses or shoplifting. Did she have any idea how many kids were into that now? And no, he wasn't dealing. He was working. Honest jobs. So she'd let it go.

Maybe getting some of the things he wanted would keep Roy Jr. out of trouble, though there was never an end to the things a grownup person wanted or thought she wanted, so probably Roy Jr. wanted way more than he ever got and ever would get from either his dad or her.

As Veronica came into the central downtown area she began to look for Roy Jr. The kids milled around in groups of three, five or six. Mostly it was slim young boys in their baggy, funny-looking pants. Bein' cool, pants hanging on hip bones, big shirts, caps, and some with wool tuques pulled low on their brows. Girls too, same styles, minus the tuques. Two-tone hair. Black and blond.

On the concrete plaza outside the mall, a group of kids with skateboards made their moves down one set of stairs, along the freeway, then up another jump of two or three stairs, along rails, arms and bodies adept at shifting weight. She watched them waiting turns, watching one another, judging, laughing, and she wondered if Roy wanted a skateboard, if he ever hung out there watching, and she thought of asking if they knew him, if they'd seen him, but she didn't ask.

In the next block, another trio moved toward her. These boys were more like Roy was now. Alert while seeming not to be, eyes darting under dropped lids. They talked from the sides of their mouths, did not look at one another. And they were rough, she thought, on the edge of aggressiveness, an inch from the edge, so the one who got pushed off the curb wouldn't be quite sure if it was a push or just horsing around. They were at each other and calling out to another group across the street outside the donut shop, sharing, by the looks of it, a joint. Veronica squinted, took off her glasses, squinted again. No Roy amongst them.

When these kids moved, they walked a walk that was like sauntering, like they were in no hurry to go anywhere, but no one had better stop them or expect a one of them to move aside. A complete and total selfishness. A complete and total lack of respect, even for the old woman with the cane and the old man who supported her. These elders flattened themselves against the building while the kids passed. Some of these kids, Veronica thought, would surely duck into a doorway rather than be seen by a granny or auntie, grandfather or uncle. Roy would. She knew he would duck. He'd been taught that much, that deep. Hadn't he? Where was he? In a doorway nearby? Or running now, toward home.

Where was he? How lonely was he? Who were his friends and why had she never met any of them? How was your day? Okay. Are you glad to be through school? I guess. Shrug. Put in an application at McDonald's or DQ. No answer, not even a shrug.

She wasn't going to find him. She'd made the rounds. Now she began to climb the hill to the high street above town, homeward on a beautiful night. Puffing a little. Enjoy, she said. The harbour, the mountains' soft peaks against the pink and blue sky. CN, the train yards, the fish docks. She'd run to Vancouver (where else to run?) when she was young, a little older than Roy, lasted a year out of pride, made it a year down there and oh God, so glad to be back where people knew you and cared a little bit, any-

ways wouldn't see you stuck on the street. Friendly. You
could have a good time without a wad of money or wallet
full of credit cards. And work. And real food, not just
Kraft Dinner. Nobody'd ever brought her a fish in
Vancouver. Sure, there were people with bad habits here,
but you knew who they were and what they were up to
got around fast so you could watch out for yourself and
your kids. And even if Roy Sr. was dealing, he'd be watching out for young Roy. He'd know through the pipeline if
young Roy was up to no good. He'd be on top of it faster
than she could be.

She ran out of reassuring thoughts at the crest of the
hill, and though it was a half a block in the wrong direction, she headed for the playground to catch her breath.

She sat in the half-moon strap seat of the swing and
pushed herself out with her tired feet, let her sandals
scrape on the patch of worn-down earth as she swung
back down. She'd taken Roy Jr. to this playground. She'd
been good to him. Talked to his teachers, kept on his back
about homework, sat down with him at the kitchen table
and read the goddamn new math books until she figured
out what he was supposed to do. *She* hadn't changed. *He*
had. She had to work. He knew that. She couldn't follow
him everywhere. He was fifteen! He wasn't a baby!

She swung higher now, pumped. The bar had been
busy last night. Packed on a summer Saturday night.
She'd been packing trays of draft for a couple of hours and
had to pee like crazy so she'd grabbed her purse, intending to take a minute to comb her hair. She went into a
stall, the end one, and squatted, didn't sit, let it drip, then
thought, ahh, and sat. Just for a minute. Lit a smoke.
From the next stall, suddenly, this incredible bawl, like a
calf.

Maaw. Maaaaaaw. *Mmmaaaaww.*

And then silence for a second or two.

MmmmaaawWWW.

If it hadn't been so loud and so desperate, it would have been funny.

What's the matter? Veronica called, getting up, flushing.

I want my Maaaaaw.

And then in came Florrie. What kinda racket are you making in here? What's the matter with you?

So it was Florrie's kid. Not a kid, twenty at least, and Veronica'd washed her hands, dug for her comb. Another bawl from the calf.

What the hell's the matter with you? Florrie demanded, rattling the door.

Please don't fight with Dad, the girl cried. He luuuvs you.

Tears sprang into Veronica's eyes and though she was ready with her comb, she couldn't look into the mirror. She'd left Florrie alone with the girl, who said she would not come out until her mother promised, prrommissed not to fight.

What else would arrive out of the blue sky? Up and up, her stomach butterflies on the down swing, hopeful on the up. Or was it the other way round? It didn't matter. Glimpses now of the trails leading up from the waterfront, the flattened grasses, burnt-out bonfires, and a group sitting round. As she swung down, she closed her eyes and said to herself it was Old Gordie, and Ticker and Wilf and that crazy guy who argued with himself. She swung up and saw, though she could not see that far, that it might as easily be her Roy and a couple of the kids she'd seen downtown. Passing a bottle, a joint, God knows what else.

She saw them in groups, in different spots, along different trails, hidden in amongst the alder and the salmonberry bushes, the broken glass, the needles, and she saw them look at their fancy black divers' watches and rise and start to come up the bank, through the long grasses, the fireweed, the wild daisies and horsetail on trails she and her two Roys used to take down to all the seafest activities not so long ago.

She stopped pumping, dragged her feet until the swing slowed down enough for her to jump off. She would go home now.

Last night around this time, Mike, the bar manager, had taken a walk in the middle of his shift as he usually did, just poking his nose into the other bars, checking to see who was where, which bar had the crowd, whether they had their share. And coming back from his rounds, coming along that first street above the harbour, he'd said, he couldn't believe his eyes. He said young kids started coming from every direction, closing in. Girls too, he said, weaving in and out, excited, bumping the boys' hips with their own slim hips. He said he'd thought it was a street dance happening, and memories came back to him of Main Street closed off in the summer, the different bands jamming on a flat deck. He'd thought it made a lot of sense to move off the main drag. 'Member the jerk? he'd said. 'Member that song "Do You Luv Me"?

But what was happening, he said, was these kids were herding a kid who was trying to run away, and they got him closed in, blocked on all sides, and moved him into the centre of the ring. He was just a small kid, her boss said, just a small kid (not Roy, not Roy, she'd thought) and they took turns pushing him back into the ring when he tried to get out, and her boss had hollered

Hey, what're you doin', but they ignored him. A woman yelled from an apartment window that she'd called the cops. They played the boy back and forth in the circle until he fell and then they kicked his ribs and his groin, his face, stood him up, and pushed him across the ring again. When the cop cars arrived everybody scattered over the banks. Mike couldn't believe how fast it all went down. Maybe he hadn't yelled loud enough. He'd been shaking when he told them he felt ashamed of himself for not jumping in the second he understood what was happening to that poor kid.

And everyone was quick to tell him, No, are you crazy? You'd be on a stretcher alongside that kid right now.

Veronica had called home as soon as she heard the story but Roy hadn't answered. When the night was over, all the people out the door, and the staff'd sat down for drinks, she'd called again before she sat down with hers. Roy wasn't home then either, so she'd had another drink and phoned Roy Sr., but of course he wasn't there. So she'd had another drink. Time went so fast after hours.

When she got home in a cab around 4:00, Roy was in bed, under the covers, his pants on the floor, his shoes kicked off, one here, one there. She'd crashed on the couch and then slept late and had to rush around to make it to work by noon today.

And now here she was at home again. The door was unlocked, so Roy was either home or he'd gone out, forgotten to lock up. Roy? she called softly, not sure she wanted him to answer, not sure how to begin. She looked around the kitchen, dishes in the sink, cupboard doors open. It was a cozy house when it was tidy. They had comfort there. She still hadn't closed the door, hadn't moved. Roy? she whispered, and closed it.

She tiptoed to his closed bedroom door, turned the handle and there he was, lying on the unmade bed in his pants and shoes, no shirt. Headphones on, eyes closed. Roy? she said. Roy? Louder. He opened his eyes and looked at her, then closed them again. She was not yet prepared to step over the threshold. Roy! she screamed, and he turned, rolled over lazily, stretched one arm out and with his palm swung the door shut.

Where were you last night, she yelled, pushing the door open, grabbing the headphones and tossing them, standing hands on hips, wanting to grab him by the hair and stand him up and smack some sense into him. She hadn't wanted to do it this way, she had promised herself she wouldn't get hysterical, but there she was. Were you? She put her face an inch from his. Were you part of that gang?

He looked at her, a long cool look, closed his eyes again, let his lids fall, and in his low, changed voice said, Where were *you*?

I want the truth, she said. Tell me the truth. Start with the truth.

Go away, he said.

She made tea, but couldn't hold the cup steady. Yes, the halibut was in the fridge. She rummaged through her purse, a cigarette. Cigarettes. Had she left them at the bar? Jeezus. Oh Jeezus. But here's a little bag, a clear plastic gift bag with a drawstring. Herbal teas. Oils. A bath packet. Wanda. That's right. Wanda had been into the bar that afternoon, just back from a convention in Vegas and she'd given Veronica a sample pack. Items she was going to stock now in her shop. Give them a try, she'd said. Let me know.

Veronica ran the bathwater, calmer now. She got her robe, undressed, and stepped into the hot, tumbling water. She took off her glasses and rubbed the bridge of her nose where the impressions were, greasy skin, tired, bagged right out. A bath. And the packet. She brought it close so she could read the instructions, the fine print. *Refreshing, revitalizing colour bath. This particular mixture of natural herbs and dyes replenishes your innate power and courage.* Right. Sure.

Veronica tried to get the packet open with her fingers but her hands had no strength at all. None. Useless. Worthless. She tore at the packet with her teeth and saw then that it wasn't all her, that there was a plastic liner inside the paper packet, and it now stretched like taffy. No wonder.

She dumped the powder under the running water and she had only a second to take in the pale pink before the crystals bloomed and bled deep red.

She thought she might be having a heart attack or a stroke or maybe she was in shock. Her mind screamed, her mouth was open but no sound came. I am going to die, she thought, and in the next second she thought: Roy. The water poured out hot in waves rushing at her. Red became deep pink, then paler, then simply a blush. As her sobs came in waves and shuddered through her, she began to cup the water in her hands. She carried it, streaming through her fingers, again and again, to her face, her brow, her shoulders, until she was slowed, weakened but stronger.

Facing Up

Rain on the canvas, rain streaking down the windows, rain leaking in around the chimney, sizzling and sputtering on the stove top. Wind rattles the doors on both port and starboard sides. Gusts of wind take this boat out and back, out and back against the bladders and again, the rattle and rap rap rap.

I look up from my notebook, open on the galley table, try to think: where was I? Where was I going before that last gust of wind brought me back? Where was I going with these lines on late summer in southwestern Ontario?

I stopped writing in the middle of a sentence about milkweed standing dry, the green pods emptied, the silky seeds blown away and just the silvered shells dangling from the stalks. I was cutting across dry fields down to the trickling creek. I was going to walk the creek back to the lake, follow its winding path. I was going to take off my sneakers and roll up my jeans, but then I thought of all the water bugs, the leeches and that turtle, one time. I had come along that far in these pages, gone back to age ten when I walked the creek alone, every day. I had not begun to explore the reasons.

But that last gust of wind, and the flap flap flap of the torn flag on the old boat tied behind this one I live on, has lifted me out of the fields. Where to? I don't know if I've simply returned to the present, to this place, this galley table, this town. No. Not here. Where am I? Why am I waiting? Why is it so familiar to rise from my notes and turn the oil stove up a notch and put the kettle on?

I am back at Tide Island. The wind has carried me back there. No, not just the wind, but the combination: the wind, the kettle, the notebook, the waiting. It is eerie but okay. Eerie but okay to land here, to go back. The wind and my notes will take me out. I will rescue myself when I need to come back to this galley, this boat tied up in town. I am not far away, only three or four hours by boat. I am as close as a gust of wind.

For now, I'll work at my little chipped formica-topped table in the teacherage, work but wait too. When I rise from the table to put the kettle on it will be for my nightly visitor.

I can hear him already, shuffling down the narrow gravel road that runs from one end of this bay to the other. I hear him call back to the men standing outside of Gunnar's boatshed. "Catch you later," he says. "I gotta see the teacher before she goes to bed mad."

I am so cool, so distant, so careful when he comes. Sven—dressed for rain, indistinguishable from the shiny dark, oilskins dripping, his eyes alive with the light of my coal oil lamp and the whiskey nipped from a flask in his jacket. Is this one of the nights that he's nipped all day in his boatshed?

There is a looseness about his voice and his body. Is it hope? He thinks his loneliness has gone away. We are both stray dogs. He thinks we will adopt each other, run together. I have to be careful. It is a lonely place. I wait for his visits but if my voice is too kind, if I ever cook a meal, if I by chance brush too close to him, he will think I am offering him comfort, a dry place to dry out. He will think I am his.

I am a runaway. A recluse. I asked for this and I got it. I have been running for a long time and I picked this place at the edge of the world to stop, to learn my own loneliness. In the ordinary world it is too easy to pick someone, be picked, call it love. It is only a bandage that falls off.

I have run to the edge of the world in order to go back into it whole. It will take nine months, the school year. At the end of it, I will be ready to love from a real place, not this place and not from need.

Sven isn't dangerous. He hasn't a hope of getting to me because he needs so much to be loved. His need is written all over him even when he tries to hide it with rough words, guffaws. I like him best when he talks about his work in a specific hour-by-hour, day-to-day way. How he put three rounds of planking on the stern of Robert's boat, how he patched the bow of Norberg's boat. When he talks about how he's come back to this island, brought his kids back, come back with them to open up his grandfather's shed again, the bitterness comes back into his voice and he takes another swig from his flask.

He circles but he is no threat. He cannot get to me no matter how he tries.

The wind carried that word *teacher* down the road a little ahead of Sven's boots. "Better go and see teacher before she gets mad."

The visits are always the same. When he comes, he sits opposite me in the one-room cabin. I make tea. After he leaves I make another cup and add brandy. The Courvoisier is under the sink in this teacherage, amongst the soaps and scrub brushes. It lasts a long time, not sharing.

He sits facing me, his back to the window, the road and the tide river. He says, "The tides are really low tonight." That means if anything happened, no one could get to us.

"We're high and dry again, then," I say.

He laughs a kind of phlegmy laugh and pulls the flask from the inside pocket of his oilskins. "Not dry," he says. He pours a little whiskey into the mug of tea I've set out for him and reaches for one of my tailor-mades. "If you don't mind," he says. I don't mind but I don't say. I take one myself and he reaches across to light it with his stainless steel Zippo.

He shakes himself. Some of the rain falls on the children's papers, their earnest fat-pencilled ABCs, rubbed and smudged. "Sorry," he says sheepishly, wiping them with the sleeve of his sweater. "Sorry teach." I feel sorry for him. I don't want him to apologize for an accident, for something he couldn't help doing.

He shuffles through the papers till he finds his little girl's work. He makes an exaggerated guffaw, then wipes his mouth with his sleeve. "She's not making much head-way, is she. Jeezus. Can't even make a round circle yet."

Treena is my favourite of the eight children I try to

teach in the little one-room schoolhouse one abandoned house and one empty lot down from me. My favourite, except for Joey, who draws pictures of life here in infinite detail: clotheslines and wheelbarrows and boats with every line and pole and pulley. I try not to let him see me watching him learning about himself and his world. I love his clear green gazing from window to page, back and forth. Treena's tiny hands are busy busy busy. Skittery. She is quick like a new frog. I cannot settle her unless I read her a story. Nothing else calms her. I see what mothering would be like and sometimes I wish for that title, not "teacher." I wish they weren't Sven's children. I wish myself away from this place, any escape.

"Well, Joey's all right," Sven says. "What's wrong with Treena?"

He asks as if I should know, as if I am a teacher. I can't say I don't know and I can't tell him how much I admire both his motherless children. How one seems purified, saintly, seems to move to an internal heavenly tune and how the other, how Treena seems in constant motion against what she hears. If he knew how much I thought about the three of them, it would be dangerous.

"What it is," I say, trying the answer for how it sounds, "is small muscle co-ordination. Sometimes it develops early, sometimes late."

"Well, Treena's pretty goddamn late."

"She's very bright," I say. "She has so much desire to... You can see how much she wants to go to school, to be with the other kids, keep up to them. It's just, I don't know, it's hard for her to settle, to concentrate and she gets frustrated so easily. Be kind to her. Be tender."

"How in Jeezus name can I do that if she won't let me get near her," he says. "Women!" he says.

"She must miss her mother," I say. "Joey too."

"Yeah well," he says. "Treena swearin' at you any more? You send her home if she does. She can help me in the shed if she can't behave in school." He blinks, wipes his mouth with the back of his hand. "She's like her mother. Exactly like her. Marianne didn't die from cancer. She died from being high-strung. That's what gave her cancer in the first place." He wipes his mouth again and asks, "Wanna game of crib, teach?"

"No," I say. "Not tonight. I want to be alone for a while."

"Women!" Sven says, pulling his oilskins on. "Women!"

It has been clear to both of us that we are friends, but tonight he asks for a kiss in that rough needy voice. Tonight he reaches for me, and I move away as fast as Treena moves from my touch when I try to lay a calming hand on her shoulders that rock back and forth, back and forth against the back of her desk.

"You'd better go," I say.

"Sure thing, teach," he says, looking at his watch. He reaches for one of my cigarettes, lights it and blows the smoke to the ceiling. "I had to be on my way anyway." But he sits down again and takes another deep pull on the cigarette, then stubs it out in his saucer. "I stopped by to tell you something I thought you should know, that's all."

"What should I know?"

"We all want you out of Tide Island," Sven says. "There's a meeting at the school at 8:30. We don't know what you are but you're sure as hell not a teacher."

"Go," I say. "Go to the meeting. I'll be packed and ready to leave before anybody counts the votes."

I follow him to the door, a safe distance behind, and

when he ambles down my slippery wooden pathway and turns onto the gravel road, I draw the bolt.

I am not a teacher. I will never be a teacher. I was hired because no one else wanted to fly into isolation. They needed someone to create a schoolroom atmosphere for the eight young children whose lessons come in brown envelopes from the Ministry of Education, correspondence division. The lessons come in and go out on the tide with the seaplane, once a week.

I have a degree with no real major—some literature, some philosophy, home-ec in place of a science, a half credit in eastern music, my Ravi Shankar phase when I wanted to learn to play the sitar. I loved the places a performance with sitar and tambura took me. We had to write an essay about the movement of the music, compare it to the act of making love. I got an A. The professor asked me to come to his office; he took my hand and read my palm. He said my head line was weak but my heart line was strong. I dropped the course. My heart told me to run.

Tonight I rehearse my departure from Tide Island, but I won't leave the kids without saying goodbye. I'll put in one more day at the school, then take the mail plane the next day. I hope it won't storm. I hope and pray for good weather so the plane can land. I'm both glad and sorry that I'm being run out. I celebrate with another tea and brandy. Sometimes I cry and sometimes I laugh.

In the morning, all eight kids come banging on my door. "Teacher's sleeping, teacher's sleeping," they're yelling. "Get up, get up, get up," they're calling, dancing around the cabin. I give the oldest boy the key. I pull on my jeans, sweater and boots and meet them at the schoolhouse and we start the day, almost on time. I want to say goodbye but somehow we just carry on as usual except that I ask them what they'd like most. They want me to read more chapters in *The Lion, the Witch and the Wardrobe*. When we get to the part where the lion dies we are all crying and I close the book. One of the big boys protests. He says we've got to go on now, got to read to the end.

At 3:00, the kids run off. While I am tidying, wiping the blackboard, I am smiling about Treena. Lately she's been making deep gouges in her desk top, she's been ripping her papers into pieces, storming out of the classroom saying, "Fuckin' ABCs, I'm going to the boatshed." But she stops her storming once she's in the cloakroom and waits for me to call her back. Today I had an inspiration, a last-day inspiration, that she would work better on a big surface than on a small paper, cramped between lines and interlines, held tight by them, so I invited her to work on the blackboard. Now there are big circles and small ones in all the colours in the chalk box, bubbles all over the board. She was happy, engaged, for almost an hour— longer than I'd ever seen her stay with a task.

I hear a throat clearing and turn to see Sven. "I'm sorry," he says. He has slipped in, sits in a desk at the back of the room near the piano. His head is hung low. He's slumped into himself. "I'm sorry. I lied. I made the meeting up."

"That's okay," I say. "I was going to leave this place anyway. I quit." And I did quit, took the mail plane to town the next morning.

Now I live on this boat, at the edge of town, and I work at the post office. I went to Tide Island to learn to live with myself. I am still learning. I live rent-free on this old boat at the shipyard. The owners of the yard like to have someone around to keep an eye on things at night. There's never been any trouble.

I have quit several jobs since coming here but now I think I have found the perfect place to work. Finally I can rest for a while. Finally I am happy. It is good on a night like this. It's good on a night like this to know my work and to welcome it.

The storm tonight has taken me out and back from everywhere my life has taken me. I have only begun to put it on paper. I have only begun to consider when I want to pin and pen things, places, people, myself. And if, how? How to pin and name and yet leave us all free and floating, capable of changing our lives a little.

At the post office I stand at a long table heaped with letters and parcels. I wear an olive green bib apron and I do a job called "Facing Up." I turn letters stamp and address forward, and put them in bins. I check to see if the postage is correct for destination. It is exactly what I need to do. Like the storm, it takes me out and back from everywhere I have gone, everything I have been. I float. Certain handwriting, that of someone very old or very young, touches me. Certain names, addresses. Sometimes my eyes water.

Sometimes I sort and bag mail for the coastal villages. The bags go out on trucks down to the seaplane base. Sometimes I see the 9x12 Ministry of Education correspondence envelopes going out and coming back. Once I saw Treena's name and address in the upper left hand corner. Her printing is a little scratchy, like bird prints, but it's there, her own marks in the corner. The *a* is round, the stem's touching the circle. Before, she used to put the straight line too far away. She didn't seem to know how to put the circle and the line together, or if she did, her line extended too far down, extended out of the line she had to work on. But I think she's got it now. She's on her way.

Until tonight, I've just imagined myself flying over Tide Island with the pilot and the mail. I imagine flying over with the mail, handing the bag to the boy in the skiff, exchanging the incoming mailbag for the outgoing mailbag and flying back. In my imagination, I say to the pilot, "Should we go to Mexico? Should we get fuel and circle Mexico?" Until tonight, I haven't wanted to revisit the teacherage, myself, or the island. This is my first visit. I put the kettle on. There's brandy under the sink in this boat. I'll celebrate.

How can I explain? Returning pleases me in the same way filling notebooks pleases me. Sometimes I just make a row of perfect flowing ohhhhhs.

Not long ago I found a type of pen that I like very much. It encourages me to write about my travels. It reminds me of the old-fashioned fine-nibbed fountain pens.

I am too young to have used bottles of ink at my school desk but old enough to have sat in wood easel-topped desks with inkwells. We would set a cup in the well or roll up our scribblers and poke them into the hole. No. Let me take time in this journey back to write it right.

Some of us set cups in the well and arranged pencil crayons from light to dark in the cavity of the cup. Some of us took such good care of our pencils, our crayons, our colours. Other kids' pencils had bite marks, teeth marks all over. Most boys needed half a dozen erasers from the back cupboard where all the supplies were kept. Most girls needed only one or two for the entire year. I was one of the girls who got the answers all right. One pearly pink rubber lasted me all year.

But there must have been some point where I started erasing, where there was no answer that felt right any more and I am going back to find that point. I am on my way.

I've turned a page. Several pages. I have to look back to see where the wind was blowing me before I put myself on Tide Island. I forget. Was it Woodstock or San Francisco with flowers in my hair? Was I going to sit at Dylan Thomas's grave or had I just come back from Wales?

I was walking the creek when I started tonight. I was lonely in those fields but I love them.

I don't want company. I am glad the rattle and rap, rattle and rap, is only wind.

Colouring

Tonight, Joe and I and Julie and Jeremy sat at the kitchen table colouring. We worked together on one picture. How often does this happen? Almost never. When the kids were younger, I used to set them up with paper and paints and brushes, and sometimes colouring books and crayons, but I didn't colour with them. It was a way of setting them aside so I could do something else, the way you turn on "Sesame Street" or cartoons and say "Don't bug me for a while."

When we linger at the table now, one of us will take a pen from the mug on the window sill and begin drawing a moustache on a town councillor pictured on the front page of the Daily Snooze. Talk carries on around the doodler. Sometimes it's contagious and soon we're all working away on scraps of paper making intricate designs that can't be interpreted.

Tonight was different.

Jeremy won a prize at his school today—a doodle art set. He won, not for guessing the number of jelly beans in the big pickle jar by the office, though now he thinks he'll win that too, but for "Kindness to his Grade One Classmates." His teacher told me she didn't think he had a mean bone in his body. I pretended to study his research report on alligators, biting my lip so the tears wouldn't fall.

He brought his prize—ten felt pens and a poster-size picture of jungle life—to the table immediately after supper. Within seconds Joe began on the stripes of the tiger; Jeremy chose the parrot's tail and Julie tackled the elephant. She *is* a tackler.

"Pass the green," I said, "I'll do leaves."

And for a half hour, until the kids started fighting about which of them needed the yellow most desperately, until Joe yawned and said he thought he'd have a snooze, we were one heartbeat. The slate was clean. For a half hour there was nothing to want, nothing to seek, fear or envy. It's the way I wish going to church could be. God was there in us. We were one spirit and one body.

We have only coloured together one other time. It was one of those nothing-ever-happens nights between Christmas and New Year's and it was a defence tactic, something Jeremy reached for by instinct. Who knows, maybe he'll win the Nobel Peace Prize someday. My ambitions for my family creep in, creep up on me. It surprises me how fierce I am.

Pass black, Joe, I'll do tiger now.

I blacked out that night, hours after the kids had gone to bed. For two days, the two days of hangover, I felt both humbled and fierce. Ashamed but enlarged by my fierceness. For two days, nothing but bread, clear tea and clear-eyed children. On the third day I moved back to toasted bagels, with just a little cheese, equilibrium returning.

I had a turkey soup simmering on the stove and while the kids and I waited for Joe to come up from the dock, we watched the flakes falling from the black sky, beautiful, dizzying, covering the soggy brown and green yard, the cedars, the salmonberry bushes, the sidewalks. I promised the kids we'd go out for a walk after supper and if enough of the white stuff fell, we'd make angels.

There was a knock at the door and Julie and Jeremy both ran through the living room to the front porch, hoping it would be someone bringing them a post-Christmas parcel. The door opened to a big man, bearded, in a light grey suit. He spoke to them and then they shuffled behind one another, the exact opposite of how they'd approached the door, elbowing to get ahead. As I walked toward them, I recognized the man. Frank. Frank? Frank Thomas.

I didn't know him. I knew *of* him. I had heard of his wealth, had driven by his home, a modern fortress, huge and almost windowless on the side facing the street. I'd studied it and the other houses on the high waterfront bluff from the perspective of the railroad tracks below, had often walked there with Joe and wondered if a view of the harbour would give us more insight, wisdom or peace.

The snow fell on Frank's hair and shoulders, and he knocked his black toe rubbers against the door frame. I invited him to step inside, come in out of the blizzard.

"No, no," he said, gesturing to the street. "Car's running. Is this Joe's place? Joe Olafson?"

"Yes," I said. "He's down at the boat. He should be back any minute."

"Are you the wife?" he asked.

"Yes," I said. "Fran."

"Well, Mrs. Joe," he said, "tell him I'll be back. You tell him Santa's coming to see him tonight. You people have your dinner. Tell Joe he should fix this porch light. And the screen door too. You tell him Santa's coming tonight."

We tidied the house. The kids were glad to help; after all, Santa was coming, right? Joe sliced some smoked salmon into thin slivers and I put it on a glass plate shaped like a fish and set some crackers around the edges. I was going to lay out some of Joe's dad's pickled salmon in a dish too but Joe said not to bother. "If Frank wants to try it, set the jar on the table and give him a fork."

I laughed. "He's rude," I said. "Something. Something about him bothers me."

"He's a character," Joe said. "You don't have to like him."

I saw something in Joe then, maybe not nervousness, but a tightening in his jaw like he had thought of all the things he might say and decided not to say any of them.

"Frank's older than you, isn't he?" I asked. We were sitting at the table by this time, waiting. "How would you explain him? Con artist? Hustler? Self-made man?" Joe looked at me as I picked up speed. He put his hand up like a policeman at a crosswalk. Was he holding a stop sign or just wearing a white glove? In any case, I stopped.

Frank came straight through to the kitchen with a liquor store box. He set it on the table. "Ho, ho, ho," he said.

"What's this?" Joe asked.

"Take a look," said Frank.

Joe flipped up the cardboard flaps and inside there were twelve bottles. He lifted one out, set it back in. And then Frank took over, setting each bottle out on the table.

"Demerara," Frank said. "Jamaican spice. Light. Dark. Navy. Amber. White." When he'd finished he tossed the box into the corner.

For some reason, I imagined a bird in a cage in that corner: a canary. I saw the bird startle, the cage swaying on its spindly stand as if it might topple. I heard birdseed slide on newspaper, felt my toes grip my sneakers like bony feet on a perch.

"I'm gonna have one drink with you folks," Frank said, "and then I'm gonna run. The wife's waiting. Joe," he said, "you did me a turn and I thank you. Mrs. Joe," he said, "get the glasses. Will you join us for a drink?"

Frank owns a logging company, or used to. He made his money and got out, then linked into development or real estate or whatever people do to keep their money making more money. A few years ago he bought an old wooden packer and put her into the shipyard for a year's worth of work, inside and out. It's a beautiful boat, a pleasure to look at.

A group of tourists, men from Japan, came into town last fall. They were walking the docks looking for someone to take them on a two-week fishing trip when they spied Joe working on his engine. They wanted something out of the ordinary, an adventure. They could pay big bucks. Joe walked with them along the dock to the finger where Frank's boat sat, and pointed. "Just for the hell of it," he said, "give the guy who owns that old packer a call. I don't know if he charters, but he might."

"He was the best guy for what those guys wanted," Joe'd said. "I thought about it. I thought about who'd show them the time of their lives. Take chances, like. Chances some of the other operators wouldn't. That's what those guys wanted."

"I always return favours," Frank said. "It's good for business and it gives me pleasure. What goes around comes around, eh Joe? I got that boat working for me now. Hell, I thought the wife and me would spend our summers cruising but she gets seasick. I got Gordon Emery running it and we're in business. You want a job, you got it. Mrs. Joe, get those glasses down and I'll set them up."

He gave a jolly order. Ho, ho, ho. Nothing wrong with that, I thought. So why was my heart beating so fast? Why were the kids shuffling around me, trying to hide from him, yet peeking out from either side of me, trying to see him? It was ridiculous.

"Is there anything for me?" Jeremy whispered as I got out the ice.

"No," I said. "This is Dad's time for a present. Dad's present." I had the glasses and the ice cube trays pressed against my breasts, the kids pressing in behind me. It was hard to walk.

"This is your wife," Frank said. "You have a wife, you have two children. Introduce me."

I wanted to turn down the heat. Turn down the lights, bring out the little Christmas tree from the front room, the little tree with the blue lights that blinked on/off/on/off. Anything to cut the glare of the sunlamps this guy had turned on us.

"Slow down, Frank," Joe said. "I was just getting to that."

Both kids continued to hide. I had never seen them behave like this. I brought them out from behind me, tucked them under my wings, made a kind of Oriental bow. I was so thirsty I wanted to grab one of the bottles and take a long straight slug from it. Why did I bow, for God's sake?

"Is this the only wife you've had?" Frank asked Joe. He bowed slightly to me, then turned back to Joe. "I gotta catch up on your life, Joe. Fill me in. You're fishing. I know that much. Got any money? You own this house? You could make something out of this place if you got at it. I know all about making something from nothing. All about it. When are you gonna take the bull by the horns and tackle this place?"

I waited for Joe to speak but he didn't. I was confused by his stubborn slowness. I wanted him to restore the natural light in the house, but he didn't. Wouldn't. Couldn't. It made me want to machine-gun Frank. Arm us all. We'd gun him down. *Ratattatattatatat*. Gun him down.

"Just a light one for the lady?" Frank asked, looking at Joe.

"No," Joe said. "She probably wants a stiff one."

Jeremy and Julie sat in the chairs farthest away from Frank, between Joe and me. After a minute or two, after Frank had turned his headlights off Jer, having asked him how old he was, was he tough? was he smart? did he like the girls? Frank directed his attention to Julie. "Little Miss," he said, bowing. "Hello little Miss."

Jeremy slipped out, ducked under the table and slid back in with a colouring book and crayons. He climbed onto my lap. With quiet care Julie turned the pages until she came to a farmyard scene that stretched across two pages—the house, the barn, chickens pecking, a dog romping, a boy, a girl, each with an overflowing pail of grain, a cow, a horse. Jeremy dumped the box of crayons and the kids began on the animals. I chose a summer green and worked on leaves.

Joe kept an ear tilted toward Frank but his eyes were drawn to the paper farm. His fingers tapped on the tabletop keeping time to Frank's patter or to a tune in his own head or both. He took a deep drink, asked Frank if he'd had a good Christmas, picked up a blue crayon and started on the sky with short, even strokes that ran from the roof of the barn to the edge of the page. Julie, Jeremy and I adjusted ourselves to make room for him.

Frank said he'd had a nice Christmas. So much god-damn junk around now you couldn't walk through a single room without tripping on something. "I got one of those video cameras for the wife. That's what she wanted and that's what—" He stopped mid-sentence.

"What the hell's wrong with you people?" he yelled. He actually leapt up from his chair. "Did I come on the wrong night or what? You don't like my company? You always *colour* when you have visitors? I've never seen anything like it."

I had to give Frank credit for that. It was strange, and he'd broken the tension. Joe said, "Tell me how you made out with that charter last fall." He poured himself and Frank and me another shot. I took the kids up to bed after that second drink, promising snow angels in the morning.

I thought about having a bath, going to bed, but I didn't want to. I wanted to go back into the bright light, back to the Demerara. I told myself I was curious, that I would amuse myself, keep colouring and listening up there in the leaves looking down on the scene. I would be like Joe, enjoy the unfolding of this "character," Frank. But it wasn't just curiosity. I wanted to go back and set things straight. I wanted to reclaim the power in our house.

Joe had brought marine charts up from the basement, put leaves in the table. The charts were rolled out in full, a bottle of rum set down on each corner.

Joe knows the coast like he knows his own hands. He wasn't talking much but his face was relaxed, amused even, as he listened to Frank's tales of all the tricky coves, shallow spots, reefs and rocks not marked on the charts. We listened to Frank run down and praise the Japanese in the same breath. Slope heads, slant eyes, smart, quick, bright friendly little buggers. They'd had a good time on that charter, and so had he. Best time he'd had in a long time. They all gave him their addresses and they told him if he ever went to Japan, they'd treat him like a king. He thought he'd make that trip pretty soon. He'd heard about what a man could get in some of those countries and he didn't want to pass that up. Life was for living, wasn't it? Eh Joe? And a wink. And a glass raised to me. "Mrs. Joe."

We drank one bottle from a corner of the charts and set a new one down. And on it went. Frank asked for a little music. Why didn't we put some music on. He started to sing that one about the muddy river on the mighty Mississip.

He said his father was a mountain man. Never liked too many people around him. His mother was a beautiful lady, he said, out of the ordinary beautiful, but she didn't like the bush and his father couldn't tolerate living in town. He tried to keep his fancy wife but he couldn't, and they parted. His mother got religion and his father got lost in the bush. Frank would run away, find his dad and sleep in peace under bear skins, and every time, Children's Aid would track him down, round him up and take him back to sheets and cheap blankets with pictures of cowboys riding broncos.

Joe got out his guitar and he sang that one Sinatra sings about puppets and paupers and princes and men. Of course Frank thought that song was meant for him, written for him alone. He was grinning ear to ear. And Joe had a big grin then too. He was satisfied: he had Frank's number, all right, and he was satisfied. Frank was satisfied. There they sat, singing and satisfied. It would have been a good time to pass out cigars.

I should know I'm getting drunk when I want to sing "Satisfied Mind." It's the only time I think of that song. "How little they know that it's so hard to find, one rich man in ten with a satisfied mind." I do remember humming the melody until Joe found the lyrics.

Money can't buy back
Your youth when you're old
Or a friend when you're lonely
Or a love that's grown cold.

And I remember being so happy that old Frank was singing his heart out too. But I don't remember anything else. Nothing. Black.

I woke up early. The sun was streaming through the bedroom windows and there was the bright, blinding bright white snow. I felt great. Like I'd lost ten pounds, got a new heart.

"Joe," I said, nudging him awake. "Joe, I feel so good."

"Yeah?" he mumbled. Hmmm. A tone there in his voice. What was it? Not just sleepiness.

"Yeah. I feel great," I said.

"Why?" he asked. That tone again.

"I don't know. I just do. What's-his-name isn't so bad after all. He's human."

"Human, eh? You don't remember telling him he was a racist pig, telling him that you hated guys like him who make a lot of money and then go to ThighLand and BangCock?" The tone in his voice was contempt mixed with resignation, disappointment.

"No," I said. "No, I don't."

"We were having a great time till we got him to the front door and then you turned on him. Frank didn't know what hit him. You attacked him. I couldn't understand what you were saying. You didn't make sense."

"No sense at all," I said, as flatly, as calmly as I could. "Nothing I said."

"You were babbling about power and oppression and sorrow and ego, a whole bunch of crap all mixed up. And to top it off, you fell off the front steps and I had to pick you out of the flower bed."

"None of it made sense," I said again. Flat and cold, my heart beating fast.

"I thought about it," Joe said. "I thought about grabbing Frank's tie and twisting it around his neck."

"So why didn't you?" I asked. "Why didn't you twist his tie around his neck?"

"I'd like to wring your neck," he said. "I thought you understood. Frank's Frank."

"Why would you strangle him?" I asked again.

"That charter, the way he talked about those Japanese guys. The way he talks about the people who work for him. He doesn't give a shit about anybody. You're both full of shit. Both of you," Joe said. "You don't change a guy like Frank. He's not gonna change."

"Well, I am," I said. "I'm gonna change."

"Sure you will," said Joe. "Me too."

"I will," I said. "You watch."

I threw the covers aside, went downstairs, and began my ascent with toast and clear tea, a clean black slate.

ACKNOWLEDGEMENTS

Stories in this collection were first published in somewhat different form as follows: "Houselife," in *Room of One's Own*; "Romeos," in *Westcoast Fisherman*; "Naming," in *Prairie Schooner* (Canadian Women Writers issue); "Colouring," in *Grain*, and "Facing Up," in *Windsor Review*. Thanks to these magazines for their support.

"Fool Such As I" was first written as a stage monologue and had a staged reading at the Women in View Festival, Vancouver, in 1992. I thank the View selection committee, director Deborah Thorne, and actor Lillian Carlson for giving me the opportunity to learn more about stage vs. page.

I would like to thank the Canada Council and The Banff School for their support.

On the home front, I would like to thank photographer Nancy Robertson for the many good talks as well as the pic. Of course and always, thanks to Tom, Maggie and Dylan.

Finally, a special thanks to editor Mary Schendlinger for her enthusiasm and insights.

For the reader who would like further information on the text referred to in "Naming," the set is titled *Na*

Amwaaltga Ts'msiyeen (*The Tsimpshian, Trade and the Northwest Economy*) and was published by the Tsimshian Tribal Council and School District 52 (Prince Rupert).

This is a work of fiction. Although many of the stories began with what is real, events, settings and characters soon departed from the real for the sake of "story."

CREDITS

"Christian Island (Georgian Bay)" by Gordon Lightfoot, © 1972 Moose Music Inc. Used by permission.

"Blue Wing" © Tom Russell, End of Trail Music, SOCAN. Used by permission.

"Famous in Missouri" by Williams and Clark, © Tom Collins Music Corporation (BMI) and Collins Court Music Inc. (ASCAP). Used by permission.

"Satisfied Mind" by Joe Hayes and Jack Rhodes, © 1955 (renewed) Trio Music Co., & Fort Knox Music Inc. All rights reserved. Used by permission.

Emotions by June Callwood © 1986, originally published as *Love, Hate, Anger and Other Lively Emotions* (Toronto: Doubleday Canada Ltd.). Used by permission.